White-Noise Conspiracy

Panayotis

Published by Panayotis, 2023.

WHITE-NOISE CONSPIRACY

First edition. April 27, 2023.

Copyright © 2023 Panayotis.

ISBN: 979-8223228028

Written by Panayotis.

Also by Panayotis

Junior and Dumb Old Bo
Junior and Dumb Old Bo
Junior and Dumb Old Bo's Trip To The Olympics

Standalone
Michael
White-Noise Conspiracy

Table of Contents

This book would not have been possible without the patience
of my beautiful wife Susan

White-Noise Conspiracy

Chapter I

There is Always a Beginning

The night lit up as the massive storm caused havoc throughout Manatee County. They well named it the Tampa Bay area as the lightning capital of the world. The storm's downpour was so strong it was impossible to see two feet ahead of yourself.

Everyone left the area around Bud Rhoden Road because of the evacuation order. The authorities issued an evacuation order near the old Piney Point fertilizer plant wastewater holding homes near the old reservoir. So, they evacuated all the homes south of the plant. It had become a gold mine of places to hide!

A silhouette was moving between the abandoned homes. It slowly exposed the silhouette as a man with a white baseball cap, white tee shirt and sunglasses walked into the light that shone from one of the streetlights. After a few attempts, the man was able to find a home into which he could easily enter. He got in through the sliding French doors at the back of the home. The home was dark. He entered, and he felt sure that he was not going to turn on any of the lights. He didn't want any prying eyes to notice that someone was in this house. With the small trusty six-dollar flashlight that he had got at Home Depot, he was able to find a small desk in the makeshift office at the back of the house near the master bedroom.

He quickly took his computer out of his backpack and laid it on the top of the small desk. He then took out the computer wires and plugged them into both the computer and the router, respectively.

His old computer rumbled as it desperately tried to start up. He knew it would. It was only a matter of time. It was an old reliable computer. It has not failed him yet. He quickly opened his pocketbook to find the addresses he needed to get to his hacker link to his now notorious site.

The big red flaming V lit up the computer screen with the writing "HADES IS BACK, GET READY FOR HELL" written beneath the big red V.

He sat back in his chair took off his white and blue baseball cap and a newly shoplifted sunglasses and placed them on the desk, while looking at the screen and was very proud of himself as he grabbed his pack of cigarettes from the side pocket of his backpack. With a lit cigarette in his mouth, he sat there contemplating exactly what or who he was to transmit his virus to next. Would it be the FBI, DOJ, or even the White House?

So much degeneracy, and so little time to expose them all. He decided to expose to the World Wide Web the venality of the life and political time of our great wonderful President.

With his eyes glued to the screen of his computer, he typed in a massive number of keystrokes, as his fingers glided gracefully over the keyboard like a Prima ballerina. He was so involved with his work that he did not pay attention to his surroundings. The creaking noise of the floorboards got his attention. He turned his face, only to look down at the barrel of a gun. He was paralyzed, unable to move. His eyes slowly looked up to see the bearded face of a giant of a man that held the gun.

"Well, well, the man said. I thought you had turned to stone."

He was speechless as he glanced behind the man who stood in front of him to see a beautiful young red-headed woman and another man behind her. The man tried to open his mouth to say something, but no sound came out. "Speechless, no problem my friend. I will do the talking and you will do the listening. Understood, good?" The big man said. The man nodded in a positive way.

"My name is Shane O' Brady. This is my son Brian and my daughter Shannon, and you're Hades, right?" Once again, the man answered with a nod. He was scared and the big man still had his gun aimed in his direction. He was not sure where this conversation was going. So far it has not looked good.

"My son Brian is quite good with computers. He has been following your exploits," Shane said.

"You bet I have," said Shane's son Brian.

Shane's son Brian would have dropped like a rock If looks could kill. Brian realized he had made a major mistake. His father insisted that no one was to speak unless instructed to. The anger on Shane's face slowly dissipated as he turned to face the man. Thankfully, a smile returned to Shane's face. Shane then expressed his enjoyment of how the man could keep one step ahead of the FBI.

"My question, young man, is whether you are extremely smart or just damn lucky," Shane said.

To be honest, that question had come to the man's mind frequently. The man did not feel that he was exceptionally smart. So, then the only answer was that the FBI was extraordinarily stupid! Shane continued with his cross-examination of him that in many instances, he was unable to or didn't want to answer. This onslaught of questions just did not stop until he spoke.

"Okay, enough," the man said, "what the hell do you want and who the hell are you?"

The smile slowly left Shane's face. The thought that the man had just made a major mistake with the way he spoke was not one of his smartest moves. Shane stared at the man for a moment and then looked back at his son.

"So, Hades, what is your real name?" asked Brian as he stepped forward.

"Why do you want to know?" He replied.

Brian quickly snapped back, "if you don't answer my questions, I'll slap the answer out of you." He moved towards the man as he lifted his hand to strike.

The man quickly answered, "Juan Rodriques."

"Now, wasn't that easy to say?" said Brian.

He grudgingly nodded his head yes.

"Now let us get down to the nitty-gritty," Brian said.

Brian grabbed a chair and sat in front of Juan. He gave Juan's computer screen a quick look over and then turned his sight in Juan's direction. He sat there staring at him, waiting for him to return the stare.

"So, what system do you use to get your information?" asked Brian O'Brady. "Also, what program do you use to turn their computer systems upside down?"

Juan did not answer Brian's question. Instead, he answered his question with his own question. "Who are you all? The Cops, FBI or are you folks the neighborhood watch?"

Shane burst out laughing as his son Brian and daughter Shannon quickly joined in.

Brian stood up and replied, "We're the IRA," as Brian O'Brady continued to laugh.

"The IRA?" Juan responded. "What the hell are you talking about? We are in Palmetto, Florida, not Belfast, Ireland." Juan could not figure them out. Were they a crazy or fanatical political group?

"I knew we were not in Ireland. It was just a little too warm for Belfast," Shannon said, as she chuckled away.

Juan glanced at Shannon. She was one beautiful woman, and Juan would love to know her better if she did not laugh. Her laugh would drive him crazy. It was worse than the Vice President's hideous babbling that sounded like a hyena.

Old man O'Brady got up from his chair and walked towards him. Juan felt a wave of uneasiness crawling up his spine. He stopped momentarily while he spoke to his son, Brian. Occasionally, while they were talking, Shane would turn around and look at Juan before continuing his talk with his son. I was very curious about what they were talking about. Eventually, Shane came over to speak to Juan. He also grabbed a chair and sat down in front of me while his son Brian and his daughter Shannon stood beside him.

He stared at me quietly as he seemed to be contemplating how he was going to explain to me his proposition. He finally started to explain what their purpose for tracking me down was all about.

"I am going to try to make it simple for you, Juan, "said Shane. "We want to change Washington DC to the way it should be run."

Juan just nodded his head, hoping that Shane O'Brady would understand it, as he comprehended exactly what the hell he was talking about. Shane continued to explain the points of his plan that would change Washington, DC as we know it.

"Really, how do you plan to do that and how am I going to fit in this plan of yours? Juan asked.

Shane quickly responded, "we will, with your help, destroy this country's governmental infrastructure. We will start by blowing up the Capital building, the Senate, and the Pentagon. We will take out the squad, speaker of the house and all the rest of those commie bastards. And if we still have a few sticks of dynamite left or possibly some C-4, we will destroy the United State Treasury and the Library of Congress. There will be bodies everywhere." Shane, his son Brian, and his daughter Shannon busted out laughing. The thought of the destruction of the government infrastructure and the death of an unlimited amount of the government was the way to go. At least that is the way the O'Brady saw it.

Juan's face changed from confusion to astonishment. He could not believe what Shane was saying, not to mention that they all found the whole irrational scenario something to laugh at.

"Are you crazy? I do not want anything to do with this. Screwing up the governmental grids is one thing: killing people to advance my agenda is another. I don't and I won't have anything to do with it." Screamed uncontrollably by Juan.

Shane raised his hands as he said" Whoa, whoa, whoa, my friend. Do not get your blood pressure up." A smirk crossed his face. "We were just screwing around with you. We have no intention of killing anyone even though some of them truly deserve to be taken out. How about we just settle on tar and feather the governor of California? He is a total jerk!

Juan nodded his head in a negative fashion. "You're no fun Juan." Shane said.

"Yea, a real stick in the mud," stated Brian. Shannon nodded her head in agreement.

Juan didn't have any apprehension about the possibility that he was absolutely wrong about the way things should be done. He had a road map of stages on the way he felt they should attack and obliterate the infrastructure of the United States.

"Alright, we will devastate the infrastructure of the United States as you wanted. But I'm in total authority over the events that will follow. I want you, Brian, and Shannon to take care of finding locations for us to work out of, and our security. Does that work for you, Shane? Juan explained.

Shane looked at his son and daughter for a momentary moment and then glanced back at Juan as he nodded affirmatively.

"Well, we have one thing already bought. "Said Shane.

"Really," said Juan. What is that?"

"My son has refurbished a camper that he put on the top of it an electrical gadget that will do the job, that you can connect to the outside world and that way we will be on the move continuously so the dam authority will not be able to pinpoint us." said Shane with a smile of pride on his face.

Juan smiled encouragingly at Shane. Yet there was doubt in Juan's mind about the rationality of the O'Brady idea. But time will differentiate between fact and fiction.

Chapter 2
Let The Fun Begin

WE ALL LOADED INTO Shane's Expedition Platinum MAX SUV. Juan sat in front with Shane driving with Brian and his sister Shannon sat behind them.

"Dam nice car, Shane, what does this SUV retail for?" Juan asked.

"They go for around $82,500 for this model. As you can see, it is very spacious, it can seat eight people. "

Juan responded," Well, it is nice to have that much capital to purchase this SUV. I can't even manage to get enough money together to buy a bike."

"Who said we purchased this car? What we did was take it out as a scrounge. "Said Shane.

Brian belted out as he was laughing," Yea, we'll pay them next week for what we misappropriated today."

"Are you telling me that you guys ripped this SUV off the bloody dealer's car lot? Are you guys crazy? Every cop around will be looking for this car."

Shannon quickly stated that they had changed the license plate from another car. No one will figure it out.

Juan was starting to get nervous again. He was contemplating the thought of how to try to get away from these guys before they were caught. He didn't get much of a chance to figure out a plan when they turned into an alley and then into a back lot that was well hidden from the main street. Parked there was a beautiful camper. Shane parked the car behind the camper, and everyone got out. Juan walked to the front of the camper and was quite impressed with it.

Brian came from behind him and said, "would you like a tour of our hideout, Juan?"

"yes, I would."

"Well, follow me."

Brian unlocked the side door and walked in, with Juan following immediately behind him. Juan was very curious about the setup of the O'Brady hideout.

Inside, Brian started bragging about their hideout while giving a total breakdown of the camper.

He explained that this model is a 2023 Gulf Stream camper meri-lite ultra lite 241RB.

It had a bunk cab, a rear private bedroom, a jackknife sofa, a shower, and plenty of storage.

Brian continued that this particular motorhome was perfect for a small family or gang depending on how you look at it. Shannon can prepare the best meal you can get. She's a great cook. It also has the continued a double-door fridge. Plenty of room for Killian.

"All the comfort of home," he stated

"It's beautiful. Did you steal this also?"

"Wow, I can't believe you said that Juan. You are destroying my self-esteem, "as he laughed.

"We didn't steal the camper, Juan, said Shane. We made the first payment and eventually we'll make the second payment, and in the meantime, we will keep it well hidden. "He continued to say that they had changed the way the camper looked like. They repainted it, changed any marking on the camper, and remodeled the inside to suit their needs.

"As you can see, we have quite a setup here. We got three large computer screens and a huge satellite that we have on the roof that keeps us connected with the rest of the world. I thank the great god of the internet to keep us safe."

Juan asked "Brian, who is this great god which you are talking about? "Also, what makes you think that they will not be able to triangulate your position as you get on the net? "asked Juan.

"Elon Musk, of course." We use his Starlink satellite. It works great. I made software that we can change our I.P. address at the push of a button as our connection travels throughout the world. If the authority starts trying to trace us, they will find us in Panama, then we will be in Argentina, Paris, France, Brussels, Belgium, London, England, or maybe even Dubai. I really have no control over where it goes. It travels throughout the internet and takes the path of least resistance."

"Okay, move over and let me grab a chair and let me try this thing out to see how good your setup is." Juan grabs his computer out of his knapsack. In no time, he was able to connect to Brian's system as he opened up multiple links to his HADES IS BACK, GET READY FOR HELL hacker system. His fingers skated across the keyboard at lightning speed and his eyes lit up as he realized he was getting closer to being able to send his fresh attack on the President.

Brian was standing behind Juan as it amazed him at the speed he was typing hundreds of keystrokes as photos of the president popped up. "What is the photo of the President all about?"

"According to the rumors, and accusation in the past about the president being accused of being a pervert. Putting his hands on the shoulder of young women as he seems to be bent over with his face so close to them as he seems to be sniffing their hair." Brian nodded his head as he continued to watch Juan do his stuff.

"Listen, I've got the munchies. I'm going to go across the road to the 7-11 store and get myself some chips. Does anybody else want anything?" asked Shannon. Brian stated he didn't want anything, and her father asked for a box of Marlboro. She glanced at Juan as he looked up at her and nodded his head that he wasn't interested in anything.

She closed the camper door behind her as she headed around a group of trees that were hidden behind a couple of enormous billboards across from the 7-11 store. The store was empty, with only an elderly cashier that was busy restocking the shelves. The senior gentleman looked up and smiled at Shannon as he welcomed her. He asked her if she needed any help to let him know. Shannon smiled at the elderly gentleman as she thanked him. She walked towards the chips and grabbed a couple of bags of Ripple and herself a large bottle of diet Pepsi and place it all on the counter while she waited for the man to come to the register so she could pay. Shannon stood there as she read some TikTok messages that were on her phone when she heard the door of the store open. She turned around to see four sheriffs and a couple of highway patrolmen walk in.

Shannon thought she was screwed. There was no way she could escape. She slowly turned around, knowing for sure that they would cuff her while reading her rights. She was wrong. A few of them smiled at her, while a few just said hello. She stood there paralyzed as the cashier added up her order and waited for Shannon to pay. She took some cash from her jean pocket, paid, and left the store. She sprinted across the street and as she looked back, she could see that the officers were too busy talking and buying whatever they needed. They paid no attention to her. She raced around the billboards, around the group of trees, and into the camper. "Where the hell have you been", asked her father. "We have been listening to the police scanner, and the airway is crawling with cops.

Shannon was desperately trying to catch her breath. She explained how the 7-11 was full of cops and she thought she was a goner! She also stated that there were at least three to four sheriff squad cars and one highway patrol car outside the 7-11.

They all stood there, trying to figure out what to do next.

"Let's get out of here before they find us," said Brian.

"No, we got to wait it out. At least until the cops have gone. In the meantime, we stay glued to the police scanner and then we can figure out our next move," said Juan.

Before Brian or Shannon could say anything, their father agreed they would stay until the coast was clear. As they listened to the police scanner, they learned that a semi-truck had lost control on the 275 overpass, and it went over the railing and crashed into many cars in the north direction of Interstate 75, exploding on impact. The report stated many fatalities as they were waiting for the Bayfront chopper to arrive to help with the survivors. Juan went out and checked out the area. He was back in a few minutes. He reported back that the area was deserted and there were no signs of cops anywhere. But there was a huge fire towards Interstate 75. Juan suggested they hit the road and go south on the interstate.

"Where are we going to go? asked Shane.

"We're going to hide in the Everglades. I know some guys; they are just south of Main Park Road near Tarpon Creek that runs into Coot Bay, and they have quite a setup. We could be lost there for a couple of weeks."

Brian and Shannon looked at their father to see his response, and Shane agreed. So, they started to get the camper set up for the trip. They had it all done and were on the road in less than thirty minutes. Juan decided he would drive since he knew exactly how to get there. As they drove, Brian was constantly trying to pick Juan's brain.

Chapter 3
Dam Mosquitoes

It took them around ten hours to find the site of Juan's friends after being lost for a couple of hours. Juan was cussing like a drunk lumberjack, as he believed that it was darker than a bloody graveyard, with absolutely no directional signs to help him. He could hear the loud chorus of the O'Brady family as their snores literally shook the car.

Shane's family was very lucky that night. If Juan had a gun, he would have shot them all. Nobody deserves to live through this kind of hell.

Juan stopped the car and yelled that they had reached their destination and got out while the O'Brady exited on the other side. Before they had a chance to move and turn around. Someone behind them yelled.

"You're a dead man if I don't know who the hell you are and why you are here in the middle of the night on my land." Said Scott Haugen.

Juan slowly turned around to see a group of guns aiming at him. "Why, what are you going to do, you dumb-ass redneck?" The O'Brady couldn't believe what they heard from Juan. Brian thought for sure that Juan was trying his best to commit suicide.

Scott brought the barrel of his 12-gauge shotgun and laid it on Juan's forehead. The O'Brady stood near the open SUV's door on the passenger's side with their hands up in the air. Scott raised his hand as he lowered his shotgun.

"You dumb ass, I could have shot you."

"If you had, you would have to explain to your mother that you shot your brother in the head." The two men stood there staring at each other until they both burst into laughter as they embraced each other.

"Maybe, but you don't use it anyway, and you are my half-brother," said Scott.

"Your right, the better half."

The group of men behind Scott lowered their guns, realizing that there was no danger from this group of visitors. Scott motioned Juan and the O'Brady family into his cabin. They slowly followed Scott into the cabin, with Juan shutting the door behind them.

"Everyone, this is my older brother, Scott Haugen. I adopted him because no one else wanted him"

"So why are you here, baby brother? The Law after you again? asked Scott.

"Not yet, but soon I think." Juan then gave his brother a lowdown on his plan to disrupt the country's infrastructure. That he was planning to have the government so busy chasing its tail that they wouldn't have time to find real American independent entrepreneurs like his brother and his partners. Scott asked Juan where he had found his new friends. They met last night and he and the O'Brady had basically the same idea. So, they decided to join forces. Juan's brother was a little suspicious of the O'Brady family and he let his baby brother know,

"How the hell can you trust these guys that you just met?"

"Just a gut feeling."

"The last time, if I remember correctly, that you had a gut feeling you ended up spending three years in reform school."

"Yea, you are right. But I finished high school, didn't I. Scott nodded in agreement. If it hadn't been for that, he would never have finished his high school. But Scott was still not sure about the O'Brady clan. As the brother continued to talk about old times when their mother came in. She was not only surprised but was so happy to see Juan. Juan stood up right away and gave his mother a big hug. She smiled at him with tear-filled eyes. They spoke for a bit and, like she always did, she got up and started to make breakfast for everyone. Juan introduced her to the O'Brady family. She smiled at them and welcomed them to their home.

"Please make yourself at home. I'll make some home cooking for you all."

Shane O'Brady, his son, and his daughter smiled and thanked her for her hospitality. Shannon jumped up and said," Please let me help you. I'm pretty comfortable in the kitchen, okay?

"Thank you. That would be very helpful. And just call me Ma. Everyone else does. As you can see, there are quite a few of Scott's friends that work here and help us with the family business. So, I certainly appreciated a little help."

Juan smiled when he heard about Scott's family business. It was true Scott ran a very profitable marijuana & illegal liquor business with the massive still he had hidden in the swamp.

After a huge southern breakfast of eggs, bacon, ham, sausage, and grits. The cabin smelled great with the smell of bacon and fresh coffee. Everyone jumped into this enormous feast like they hadn't eaten in a week. Juan looked around as he saw his brother Scott across the way from him, his men sitting on both sides of him and the

O'Brady clan found along his side of the long beautifully carves wooden table. Juan finished his last cup of coffee and he nodded to Brian to follow him.

Juan & Brian entered the camper together after Brian repositioned his satellite on top of the camper.

Juan said, "Brian, are you sure that we'll be able to get a proper signal from your satellite?"

"You damn right, we will. You'll be able to reach the moon if you want."

Juan looked at Brian and then nodded okay. Juan wasn't 100% sure of what Brian was saying. But he realized there was only one way to find out if it really worked. So, he opened up his computer and prepared to undermine the stock market. It took Juan a few hours to be able to break into the New York stock market algorithm. At last, there it was, and the market had just opened, perfect timing as he showed it to Brian. Brian leans over and watched the screen as Juan pushed the enter button. The computer exploded with keystroke after keystroke as Juan's program was able to slowly, ever so slowly, infect the algorithm that ran the New York Stock Exchange.

Juan sat back as a smile came across his face. He knew this would take a while. Juan got up and moved to the television in the back of the camper. He turned it on and changed to one of the business channel. Brian sat beside Juan on the couch as they listened to some stockbroker expert. They weren't sure who he was, but Juan knew that the shit was about to hit the fan. He didn't have to wait long. As the broadcaster was talking, shouting started in the background, and it intensified into total chaos. The broadcaster turned around quickly to analyze what was going on. He then reported to his television audience that there was an unprecedented sell-off of stocks.

"The stock market has gone crazy, "he yelled, trying desperately to be heard over the screams of the floor brokers, who were in total panic. The commentator said that he had to figure out what and why the stock market was dropping so quickly.

"Ladies and gentlemen, the market has dropped two hundred and fifty points, no that is four hundred and thirty points. My God, it's now eight hundred points and it won't stop. This market at this rate will most likely crash."

Suddenly, there was dead silence as a power surge of some kind killed all the lights, monitors, and the index board as everyone stood in total darkness.

"Ladies and gentlemen I have just been notified by the station that the government has closed the market at this time. Stay tuned to this station for updates as they happen."

"Wow, what the hell happened? Did you cause the market problem?" said Brian.

"Yup, what do you think of me now"?

Brian and Juan continued to listen to the station broadcaster as a huge smile came across Juan's face.

Chapter 4
Federal Bureau of Investigation

Ahuge black SUV with blackened windows drove up and entered the underground garage of the FBI CJIS Division[1] building located at in Clarksburg, West Virginia. The driver stopped at the underground entrance. Three men exited the back of the SUV one of the men held the door for a tall, slim well distinguished middle-aged man exited as the two other men stood, guard checking their surroundings. The middle-aged man entered the entrance with the three men following.

THEY FILLED A ROOM on the sixth floor with a few dozen federal agents all increasing their voices so that they could hear each other talk, which quickly drop to dead silence as a man entered with three more men behind him. The man placed his briefcase on the desk that was in front of the room. He opened his briefcase, took out some papers, and laid them on the desk. He looked up towards the agents in the room. "Good morning, I'm senior special agent Tim Horton." There was an immediate murmuring throughout the room when the agents realized that the man, that was standing in front of them was the most legendary agent at the FBI.

"I'm sure you are all up to date with the events that happened at the New York Stock Exchange. Well, I've been instructed to organize an elite unit to investigate, find, and apprehend the culprit that is responsible for this debacle." He continued to explain his plan of action on how they were going to get the person or people

---

1. https://www.bing.com/ck/

a?!&&p=474d86853bc683a0JmltdHM9MTY3NzAyNDAwMCZpZ3VpZD0wMWU4MWVhZS0wMDE1LT

Y0NjQtM2FkYy0wYzExMDE4MTY1MGMmaW5zaWQ9NTQzOQ&ptn=3&hsh=3&fclid=01e81eae-0015-

6464-3adc-

0c110181650c&psq=Criminal+Justice+Information+Services+Division+is+located+in+Clarksburg%2c+West+

Virginia.&u=a1aHR0cHM6Ly93d3cuZmJpLmdvdi8&ntb=1

responsible for this mess. First, he stated that he quickly verifies every agent's resume and history and had decided on six agents to work in this special elite force.

"I was instructed to make sure that the group would be diversified. Well, I'm sorry, but I don't care about your personal life. I will pick the best and strongest in the group, period!" Agent Horton told the group that if they do not hear their name, they are dismissed. The group was sitting there in anticipation of being one of the chosen ones.

Agent Horton picked up a sheet of paper and read out the names that he chose. "Andrew Theonidas, Peter Haggerty, Jesse Meier, Susan Sumbir, Arianne Fredline and Anne Bunker. I would like to thank the rest of you for your cooperation and understanding and please exit the room as quickly as you can. Thank you."

The group that was not chosen slowly stood up and headed to the exit. The air of discontent was hanging thickly in the room. With the last of the special agents slamming the door behind him. Special agent Horton looked up at the door and smiled at the unprofessionalism of the agents.

"Well, Let's get to work. We have to discuss a lot of issues before the day is over. I would like to discuss some of the past viruses we've dealt with." Special Agent Horton turned around and started writing on the blackboard behind him. He wrote five groups of words. The *Morris Worm, Melissa virus, I love you, my doom. and WannaCry, he explained, we considered them five of the most famous computer viruses* known. He continued explaining with a quick synopsis of each one.

"The Morris worm came out on November 2nd, 1988. Within 24 hours, it was estimated that 10% of all computers were infected. Robert Tappan Morris created this virus or worm. After we caught him and were interrogating him, he stated the only reason he made the virus was to find out just how large the Internet really was."

The group snickered as Horton continued to explain that Morris was considered one of the top hackers in history. He was the first computer hacker that was found guilty under the 1986 Computer Fraud and Abuse Act. That he ended up with three years' probation, four hundred hours of community service, and a ten thousand dollar fine.

"The Melissa Virus came out in the year 1999. I believe in March if I'm not mistaken." He explained that this virus used the Microsoft word program to spread it, which Microsoft became partially responsible for the vast spreading of this virus. Horton continued to explain that Microsoft had at that time shipped Windows 96 software compatibility test CD-ROM which accidentally carried the virus. David L Smith had created the Melissa Virus after a stripper he met in Florida. For his troubles, Smith received a ten-year sentence which he only served twenty months. He then continued with the third virus on his list.

"The ILOVEYOU virus also was spread via email. It was far more devastating than the Melissa Virus. We estimated that the ILOVEYOU virus reached fifty million users in about ten days." He also explains that many companies had taken themselves off the internet to protect themselves from this malicious virus, which included the Pentagon and the Ford Motor Company.

"Before we go on, does anybody need to take a break? No one answered. So, Horton continued.

"Okay, then there was MyDoom, which was the fastest-spreading email worm ever." He explained it was by far the most devastating worm. The worm showed up in January 2004 and then again in July 2009 when there was a massive cyberattack that hit the infrastructure of America and also South Korea. It had made a point of leaving the governmental site alone to avoid any federal involvement. We did not find the creator of this Worm virus. MyDoom seems to point toward Russia.

"The last virus I wanted to talk about today is called IWannaCry. This virus came out in May 2017. This was ransomware that hit anywhere between two hundred to three hundred thousand computers in the world. It would encrypt your files and hold them for ransom. And the only way you could get to your files is if t you would pay up to six hundred thousand dollars to encrypt the files in their computer." Horton also explained that this ransomware threat only lasted a few days. Luckily, Microsoft reacted quickly by sending out an update to combat this virus. Horton continued that unfortunately, the National Health Service in the United Kingdom, which at that time where running older systems suffered. It forced them to pay large amounts to get their files back.

"So now let us talk about our problem at hand. Our hacker is male or female or possibly both. This hacker's calling card is HADES IS BACK, GET READY FOR HELL. Cute is an understatement. Yesterday, this hacker tried to expose our president as some kind of sex pervert. He sent out many pictures with his interpretations of these pictures. I'm telling you; this guy has got some major psych issues. Which I know will lead to his downfall?" Then Horton brought up the disaster at the New York Stock Exchange.

When he finished his thoughts about the hacker or hackers, he started on his breakdown of what he wanted each agent to concentrate on.

"Andrew, I want you to team up with agent Arianne and I want you two to try to give me a complete profile

on this guy. His age, education, and whatever else you can figure out. "He then turned towards agent Peter and

agent Susan and told them he wanted them to investigate if anything unusual happened in the areas with these zip codes

34208, 34212, and 34222 sometime this week. He explained that was by far their best guess where the online attack on the

President came. Agent Horton then turned and approached agents Andrew and Arianne again. Agent

Jesse Meier stood up and glanced at agent Anne Bunker with a look of confusion on his face.

"Hey how about us, what do you want us to do?" Jesse stood there waiting impatiently for some kind of response.

"One moment, "replied special agent Horton.

Agent Jesse walked toward where special agent Anne Bunker was sitting to talk to her as they both waited for agent Horton to come over.

It took a few moments to finalize his instructions to agents Andrew and Arianne before he headed over to agents Jesse and Anne.

"Don't worry guys I didn't forget about you. I just had to speak to agents Andrew and Arianne before I forgot my thoughts" My mind is like a sponge, it absorbs a vast amount of information, but with one squeeze, all of it is gone, said agent Horton with a small smirk on his face.

"So, what do you want agent Anne and I to do?"

" I want both of you to head down towards the Florida Keys area and see if you can dig up some possible clues to this hacker." Horton stated that he had a gut feeling the hacker was in the United States. He was sure they were somewhere near the keys or even in the Everglades. I felt that the signals that went around the world were just a way to throw them off the right track.

"I want you guys to pack up and leave tonight. Try and report to me by early morning tomorrow."

Agent Jesse and Anne responded that they understood and that they would leave as quickly as they got their stuff together.

Agent Horton eyes followed the two young agents as they left the room hoping that he had not sent them on a wild goose chase.

Chapter 5
East Coast Drive

The next morning Juan didn't have much of an appetite, so he grabbed himself a cup of coffee and went into the camper and started up his computer. He just sat down in his chair as he turned on the television on the a news channel that had a local program going. Juan sat-up in his chair as he listened to the narrators, talking about what Juan 's action had created the fiasco at the New York stock market. He sat in his chair with an amazing sense of accomplishment. But he quickly sat back up as he turned to face his computer. He felt that he had them on the run, so he had to follow up with something bigger and better. He knew he could find something to mess up the system. Before he had a chance to come up with any possible idea when he heard next on the television made the synapses of his brain explode with diabolical ideas. He stopped for a moment as he heard that a renowned senior special agent Tim Horton was placed in charge of the investigation of the stock market incidence.

"Well, well, well. My antagonist is nothing short than the best that they have!"

"Hey what's going on Juan, you didn't eat anything for breakfast and your mother is a little bit worried about you might be getting sick?

"Hello Brian." He told Brian he was okay. That he wasn't getting sick, but he was bored and was trying to think on what he was going to do next to undermine the infrastructure of the United States."

"So did you come up with any brilliant ideas?"

"No, I didn't but the FBI gave me a great idea thank you very much."

Juan started to explain to Brian exactly what he was planning to do. And he felt if this doesn't screw up the enemy than nothing will. He believed that if he was successful than he would have the authorities running around in circles chasing their own tails. So, he told Brian just to sit there for a moment while he gets his ideas working. Brian sat there quietly as he watched Juan feverishly working on his special plan for senior special agent Tim Horton. The side door opened as Shane and his daughter Shannon came in.

"What the hell are you guys doing?" asked Shane.

Juan quickly brought both Shane and Shannon up to date on his plans on throwing a major wrench into the FBI communication system. And it was all the FBI fault that it will happen. They had given Juan the idea. Juan had the hack primed and ready to execute. He knew this was going to be the hack of the century. He turned towards Shannon who always looked beautiful and asked if she would be kind enough to come over and press the enter key on his computer. Shannon smiled at Juan and slowly ever so slowly came over as she pressed her firm thigh against his shoulder; and leaned over to press the enter button. The computer lit up with the words "*The Hack Has Started*, estimated time for the program to be totally enforce will be three hours and forty-three minutes. Juan stood up and turned around.

"I am definitely hungry. I unquestionably worked up an appetite with my little job. So, I'm going out to eat."

Juan opened the door and walked out of the camper with Brian, Shannon, and Shane following.

The group sat around the large outside table as Ma came outside to see if anyone wanted anymore coffee. Juan was too busy as he was finishing off his second giant Bear Claw as the rest of the group were definitely coffeed out.

"Man, I love these bear claws."

"We can see that. I'm surprised that you don't weigh five hundred pounds the way you eat," Said Shane.

"I am a growing boy; I need sustenance to be able to think great thoughts."

Shane was not impress by his comment, but Shannon and Brian found it funny as they snickered away.

Everyone was starting to get restless at the camp. There was nothing for anyone to do except

Shannon kept herself busy. She was enjoying her time with Ma. She was learning as many southern

dishes that she could remember or had the time to copy the recipes out of Ma's recipe book that was

mostly loose pages and scribbled notes. But as far as Shannon was concerned it was a gold mine of

delectable meals.

Shane poured himself another cup of coffee as he sat beside his son Brian across from Juan. He

ask Juan what if any were his plans about undermining the government. Juan smiled at Shane and

started to explain to both of them what was about to happen at any time now. Both men's eyes were wide opened as Juan finalized his story. Shane and his son Brian seem to be very impressed with what Juan had just finish telling them except they both showed a face of fear and uncertainty. Juan continued that if the hack work as he expected the whole goddam FBI department will go ballistic.

"I think we need to get ready, to move out at any time soon."

"Where are we going to go," asked Shane and Brian simultaneously.

"We will be heading to the east coast."

Chapter 6
All Hell Broke Loose

Andrew entered the room with Agent Arianne following right behind him. Special agent Tim Horton was in the corner of the room talking with a group of people when Andrew interrupted him and asked him if he could speak to him in private. They moved to the side of the room that was what Horton considered out of range of any eavesdropping. Andrew quickly brought agent Horton up to date with Hades' latest hack. Horton walked away; he was furious. Andrew could hear Horton cussing like a drunk sailor on shore leave after returning from being at sea for six months.

Andrew approach agent Horton and ask," what do want us to do?"

"I want you to contact the I.T. department and see if they have any updates on our system and an estimated time for the system to be reestablished." As he spoke Horton's phone rang, he took it out of his side pocket while walking away towards the group he spoke to previously.

Andrew went straight to Agent Arianne and told her what Horton wanted. They spoke for a moment and then quickly left the room to get some updates for Agent Horton. Andrew tried but was unable to contact the I.T. department, it seemed like the phone signals were down, so he went to the closest computer to try and somehow communicate with anyone at the home office. No luck, Andrew negatively nodded his head as Arianne stood still while waiting for what Andrew was planning to do next.

"We have no choice Arianne, we got to go to Washington."

Arianne agreed. They were soon on state road fifty as they drove as quickly as they could safely with their siren and emergency lights flashing. Andrew told Arianne that he wasn't sure how long it would take them to get to the Washington office. Andrew was pretty sure that it wouldn't take more than a few hours.

It took them longer then they had hope due to the insane traffic in Washington. They hadn't even gotten into the building when they noticed the pitch of mayhem that was in the air. It got worst as they entered the building. Voices were at a level of intensity that no one could actually comprehend what the next guy was saying. Andrew was looking for the agent in charge, so he spoke to an agent who pointed to special agent Sally Malik. They both rushed to Sally's side and told her they were here because of special agent Tim Horton and questioned her for an update on the progress or lack of progress with their system. She pointed at the huge monitor on the wall as the words spelt in large bloody red letters *HADES IS BACK, GET READY FOR HELL!*

"Seriously, it's this guy again. What the hell." Andrew couldn't believe that this guy known as Hades had attack again. He asked agent Malik if she had any idea or thoughts on how long this will take for the system to be back online? He had to report something.

Malik told Andrew to go to her desk and grab a couple of flip cell phones that are working through the cricket phone system and that these phones were not connected via the FBI security cell system. Andrew ran to pick up the flip phones that Malik was talking about and motioned Arianne to follow him as they rushed back to their car.

"Where are we going now Andrew?"

"We are heading back to Clarksburg. We have to give Agent Horton an update of the disaster of our communication system."

They were back in their automobile as they sped off on the way back to Clarksburg. They end up taking longer on the way back due to the abysmal traffic getting out of the Washington DC area. It was even worse than when they were coming to Washington. Andrew could not comprehend anyone living here. He felt the people must spend half their lives in traffic. All that agent Arianne could do was listen quietly as Andrew vented his annoyance at the situation they found themselves in.

When agent Andrew and Arianne got back to Clarksburg. They found Horton still in the same room. Trying desperately to evaluate a plan of action as Andrew and Arianne approached Horton. Horton turned and saw the two agents approach him.

"Where the hell have you guys been?" Horton asked the junior agents about their profile on the age, was he a male or female or if they felt it was a group of suspects

"We're Sorry sir, we couldn't get in touch with the head office to try and formulate some ideas to come up with a possible profile to give you. So, we decided to drive over to Washington to get some information"

"So, what did you get. "ask Horton?

"Nothing much. All that we know is that the attack was by this guy or group called Hades again."

"That son of a bitch. If I ever get this guy I'm going to ..." Arianne and Andrew couldn't make out what Agent Horton was mumbling but one thing was for certain, they didn't want to know what he had said.

Arianne walked towards Agent Horton with Andrew right behind her as they caught up the Horton. They stood there discussing a future plan of action on how to get Hades and clean up this mess.

Agent Susan and Peter walked in to see Special agent Horton, Andrew, and Arianne seating at a small table in the corner of the room.

"Agent Horton." Said Susan.

Horton turned around and looked towards Agent Susan and Peter and stood up as they approached.

"Well agent Sumbir and agent Haggerty what have you found out."

Agent Haggerty and agent Sombir explained what they had found to agent Horton and the others, which was very interesting. They told them that the area around the Bud Rhoden road that was in the 24221 area due to issues with the old Piney Point fertilizer plant wastewater an evacuation order was given out. The area was totally deserted. While investigating for anything out of the ordinary they were able to learn that only one home was broken into. They also found out that the I.P. address for that internet home is the same I.P. address from the break-in of our system by Hades. The Palmetto police made a total investigation of the home and found some prints which they ran through the database. They are contacting the owners of the home to get their prints to check against the prints they found. But there was two prints that was found that were on the Interpol most wanted list.

"Interpol?"

"Yes sir, Interpol." Said agent Peter Haggerty. He continued to expound that they are wanted for terrorism. That they blew up two police station in Edinburgh Scotland, one in Liverpool, England and they almost succeeded in blowing up Scotland Yard.,

"What the hell are they doing in Florida?" questioned Agent Horton.

"Maybe they are on vacation?" said sarcastically Agent Andrew.

His fellow agents snickered at his comment but there was no smile on agent Tim Horton's face.

"What's are their names?"

"According to the Interpol information we received their names are Shane O'Donovan and his son Brian." Stated Peter.

Agent Horton questioned Peter if there was any more of them or was it just the two of them. Peter not only explained to Horton that there was only the two of them, but also they claimed themselves to be the new IRA. Also, it seems that Interpol wasn't the only ones after them but so was unofficially the real IRA.

"Okay, that finalizes it. We're going to Florida."

Peter was instructed to get a private jet for them. He also told Andrew to get in touch with the local authority that they were coming down and what their purpose was. Before Peter moved, Anne asked him if she should pack a bikini as she snickered.

They immediately all moved in different directions as Agent Peter and Anne contacted the airport to reserve a private jet for their trip to Tampa, Florida while agent Andrew and Arianne contacted the local authority that they were coming. Their flight itinerary would be sent to them as soon as they have the final information. Tampa stated they would be ready for them. Simultaneously, agent Tim Horton was talking to Washington bringing them up to date with their plan to go to Tampa to try and flush out this so called Hade's character.

A LARGE BLACK SUV DROVE up to the hanger as a group of people got out and walked to the private jet that was waiting for the FBI agents. Agent Peter Haggerty, Anne Bunker, Andrew Theonidas and Arianne Fredline stood outside the jet waiting for Agent Horton who still hadn't arrived. They were starting to believe that their plans were changed. But before anyone spoke up they saw another SUV coming their way. It was Agent Tim Horton, agent Jesse Meier and agent Susan Sumbir.

They all disembarked and walked to the group.

"Alright, let's get this over with." Said Agent Horton.

They were in the air a few moments later. It took them a little over two hours to get the Tampa. It was a very smooth ride with very little turbulence. Agent Andrew was hoping that they were going to serve some kind of meal on the flight but no such luck. Andrew was starving! They landed at the Tampa Bay airport as the plane taxied down the runway. Agent Peter looked out the window and saw a crowd of people waiting for them. Agent Horton disembarked first with the rest of his junior agents following right behind him. The FBI agents from the Tampa Bay office approached Horton as the senior agent John Turner introduced himself and his colleagues. Agent Horton then turned around and quickly introduced his junior agents.

"We're around fifteen minutes from our office."

"Great, I want to get right on this." Said Agent Horton.

They all walked to three large black SUV, and they got in and drove away.

Chapter 7
St Augustine, Florida

"SO, WE ARE HEADING for?" asked Brian.

"We're going to Gamble Rogers state park campground which is around forty to fifty miles south of St-Augustine." Answered Juan.

Juan told the O'Brady that he had spent quite a few nights there. That it was a beautiful park, and it was around forty-five minutes to St-Augustine. And not too far off interstate ninety-five. The only problem was that they would not be able to get into the park until around three pm. But first we have to get through the back road to get to interstate ninety-five. They drove for about three boring hours with absolutely nothing in sight. The only sound that could be heard was Brian's cussing that the road was terrible and full of potholes. Juan decided to sit up front with Brian. With all the loud cussing from Brian Juan gave up on sleeping so he just might as well sit with Brian. It was close to sunrise when Brian slammed his brakes to stop the car.

"What the hell did you stop the car for?"

"Look ahead Juan. There something in the road and it's moving."

"Christ, its gators. A whole slew of them."

"Don't worry man I'll drive over them."

"Don't Brian, they may attack the car?"

"So, what I'll pulverize them all."

"And what if one gets to bite one of our tires and slashes it. Are you going to go out and change it." snickered Juan.

Brian turned and looked straight into Juan's eyes, "if that happens I'll send Shannon to change the tire, what can we do?"

Juan came up with an idea that he hoped would work. He told everyone that they had a couple of spare tires and one he had noticed was practically bald. So, he was figuring out if he took that tire and threw it in the water. Hopefully, the gators would rush to it and attack it giving them an opportunity to drive pass them all. Brian nodded in agreement. He wasn't sure if the idea had any merit, but it was worth a try.

"Alright, I'll help you with the tire."

"No, I rather you protect my back and keep an eye on those gators in case they slip behind me?"

Brian nodded affirmatively. Shannon didn't like the plan. It was too dangerous for Juan, so she moved to speak to Juan when her father grabbed her arm. She looked at him as he shook his head no. Shannon wasn't happy with her father's instruction, but she had learnt early in life not to question him. Juan quietly as he could not attract any of the gators and walked to the back of the camper and slowly ever so slowly removed the spare bald tire. Juan had instructed Brian that he was going to throw a tire, as soon as he saw the gators go after it that he should move. He would need to drive immediately ahead before the gators had the chance to head back to where they are now. Juan slowly climbed up the ladder that was attached to the back of the camper. It wasn't easy. The tire was heavy and awkward. But he made it without dropping the tire or falling off the ladder. He walked to the middle of the top of the camper and started to try and launch the tire as far into the middle of the watery swamp as he could reach. The thought of the Olympic athletes able to heave those ball and chains they threw than he felt certain that he would be able to accomplish this task. Juan threw the tire a good distance into the watery swamp as he could see the gators rushing into the water to find their savory breakfast. Brian saw the gators leave the shore as they rushed towards the tire, and he drove forward as quickly as he could as he heard a loud thump on the roof of the camper. He took a quick glance at the truck's side mirror and saw Juan holding on to the side of the camper to keep himself from sliding off. Brian wasn't going to stop so he hoped that Juan wouldn't fall off the side of the camper. Brian drove a couple of hundred yards where he was quite a distance from the pack of gators when he finally stopped the truck. He looked in his side mirror and he didn't see Juan. The passenger door opened.

"I wasn't sure if you were ever going to stop."

"Well, you told us Juan we only had two spare tires and one was with your gator friends. I couldn't take chance of losing anymore tires." Brian commented with a wide smirk on his face.

"Well, the sun is coming up so let's go." Juan turned around to see if anyone had any comments, and none were said. All Juan really cared about was an interaction with Shannon she definitely was getting under his skin. She sat there without saying anything except she had a big smile on her face as she looked at him. Juan turned back around. A large smile came across his face as a fleeting thought went through his mind. Shannon wanted him he thought. She wanted him like only a women wants a man.

It was around an hour later that they saw interstate ninety-five in the distance. There's was a Circle K gas station ahead just before interstate ninety-five. They all needed to get out and stretch. Brian stopped the truck, and they all took a well deserve break. They entered the Circle-K. Shannon went right away to the lady's room as both Shane and Brian went straight to the counter to get cigarettes. Shane had asked the woman at the counter for a pack of Rothman cigarettes, but the woman said they didn't have that brand. She said she had never heard of it. Brian knew that she wouldn't have any Rothman because it was a British cigarettes and they were hard to find. Brian didn't understand why his father always asked for a brand that he was pretty well sure that they didn't carry. Shane not pleased once again not having Rothman available, he asked the women for a pack of Marlboro. Juan got himself a bag of Fritos.

As the group were leaving the Circle K, Juan notice a Mom and Pop restaurant almost next door off the road to the Circle K. "Hey guys why don't we go to that restaurant."

The O'Bradys turned to look at the picturesque old Florida restaurant and they all nodded in agreement. It didn't take them long to get there where a young hostess greeted them and led them to a circular table and gave each one a menu. As they looked over the menu a waiter came and gave each one a glass of water with a slice of lemon and asked if anyone was ready to give in their order or did they need more time. Juan asked the waiter to come back in a few minutes so everyone would get a chance to look over the whole menu. The waiter smiled and said that he would come back in a few moments to take their order and walked away.

Shane was talking to his son as he glanced over to see Juan speaking to Shannon. Juan was leaning close to his daughter. Shane could see that his daughter was starting to get a bit infatuated with Juan as Shannon looked at him with a glitter in her eyes and a big smile as she spoke to Juan. Shane wasn't happy with the way his daughter was interacting with Juan. The relationship between his daughter and Juan did not fit in with his plans.

"Hey guys why don't you let me order for us all." Said Juan. Everyone nodded affirmatively.

The waiter came back to the table and poured everyone a cup of coffee as Juan told him that everyone was going to have two fried eggs sunny side up, some bacon, a couple of sausage patties, grits, toast and keep the coffee coming. They were all famished, and when the waiter brought the order to the table for everyone. They immediately started to eat. No one spoke, they were too busy as they devoured everything in sight. It didn't take them long to finish their breakfast.

"I don't know how the rest of you feel, but I'm stuffed." Said Juan.

Both Shane and Brian smiled as they both sat back and rubbed their belly. Shannon being more lady like agreed as she smiled. Juan motioned to the waiter if he could get the bill for everyone. The waiter gladly made out the check and gave the check to Juan. Juan stood up with the rest following him as he went to the counter paid the bill and then they left the restaurant.

They all loaded into the truck as Juan took over as the driver. He knew the way to the state park. He drove off and took the north entrance to Interstate ninety-five north. It didn't take them long to reach exit 278 onto Old Dixie Highway as they drove east, and the road curved toward the south where Juan turned left onto Walter Boardman rd. They continued east until they reached highway A1A and turned north. They finally reached the park, registered, and parked the camper within an hour. They had the camper off from the truck, plugged in the power, water, and the internet in record time. Everyone knew exactly what they had to do, and they knew they were getting pretty good at getting everything done.

"We passed a Publix a while back. We need to get us some supplies and I also saw a Bank of America across the street from Publix. I think I'll open an account so Brian can get some money out of the ATM." Said Shane.

"Exactly, we'll get some cash. We're running pretty low."

"We'll be back in an hour." Said Shane.

They got into the truck and drove off while Juan stood there wondering how they were going to open an account without the proper identification. Juan sat down in one of the folding chairs beside the camper as Shannon offered him a beer.

Chapter 8
Stupid Mistake

THE FOLLOWING MORNING agent Horton was having a briefing with agent John Turner and some of their agents in the conference room. There were a boxes of Danishes and a few boxes of coffees on the conference table from the local Panera. They all hovered over the Danishes as the meeting was about to commence when agent John Turner asked for everyone to hurry up and please sit down. As he was about to start the meeting an agent walked into the room and went beside Turner as he whispered in his ear. Turner's face turned red as a look of rage covered his face.

"Can someone please turn on the television." Asked agent Turner.

One of Turner's junior agents got up and turned on the television. The group listened to the broadcaster as he stated that at approximately 9 pm the previous evening the DHS, CIA, the Treasury department and even Homeland Security were simultaneously hacked to a standstill. No one spoke. They all sat there as they listened to the broadcaster speak while pictured behind him were bold red letters.

Hades is Back, Get Ready for Hell!

Agent Horton hung his head down as he muttered some undistinguishable words under his breath. As they watched the broadcast a junior agent came in the room and spoke to agent Turner that he a had a call from the Washington office. Turner had the call come through via the conference room's speakerphone as Turner turned to look at agent Horton. Horton sat there trying to analyze the situation and to contemplate his tentative options of action. The broadcaster finished his breakdown of the hack fiasco as Turner instructed the same junior agent to turn off the television as he was about to start speaking when agent Peter burst into the room and went to Horton to whisper in his ear.

"What, are you serious?" asked Horton.

Agent Peter nodded yes.

Horton sat back for a fleeting moment and then stood up and left the room with agent Turner and the junior agents still sitting at the conference table speculating what was going on. Once they were in the next room Peter showed Horton the message he received from their office about their request that he had asked them to check all new banking accounts by the name O'Donovan. He was notifies fifteen minutes ago that a Shane O'Donovan open a checking account in Bank of America on highway A1A south of St- Augustine.

"Okay, a coincidence?" asked Horton.

"I thought it might be until I check with the branch and found out that five thousand dollars from O'Donovan's account was missing."

"Any guesses how?"

"They found out that it was taken from their account through ATM."

Agent Horton asked Peter if that ATM had the ability to photograph depositors and anyone that withdrew any money. Peter told him that it did. The bank was checking their tapes and if they believed they found a possible culprit they would forward the photo immediately to him. Horton nodded okay but insisted that Peter notifies him immediately as soon as he gets any response. Peter nodded affirmatively. Horton turned around and went back into the conference room to bring agent Turner and the junior agents up to date with what he found out from Peter's phone call.

When Horton entered the room with Peter right behind him, he found Agent Turner on the phone. Horton sat down and waited for the opportunity to speak to Turner. A few moments later agent Turner got off the phone and turned and faced agent Horton.

"So, what's going on Tim?"

Agent Peter communicated to him what he had discovered from the Bank of America.

Turner listened attentively to what agent Peter had told Horton about the opening of a bank account under the name O'Donovan, and the disappearance of five thousand dollars that was taken out of that account via ATM the following morning. He also found out from Interpol that there was a warrant for a Shane O'Donovan and his son Brian for terrorism. The two claimed that they were from the IRA which was discovered an untruth.

"What are you going to do?" asked Turner.

Agent Horton told him that he had instructed agent Haggerty to put out an APB on Shane and Brian O'Donovan on suspicion of terrorism and also there is a wanted order by Interpol, and they are to be considered dangerous. He said that his junior agents are preparing to leave in a few moments to investigate validity of his suspicions that they have, the right O'Donovan's. Horton got up and told Turner that he would relate any updates to him as quickly as they became available. Turner told Horton to be careful and he'll be waiting for any up to date information from him.

Agent Horton joined his junior agents as they headed towards the garage. They immediately got into their car and drove out of the garage heading for the Bank of America branch for additional information. Agent Andrew was driving as he put the flashing blue lights on hoping that it would help to expedite their trip to the bank. He was wrong; interstate ninety-five was block solid with all three lanes filled with cars that were backup bumper to bumper as far as the agents could see. Agent Horton told Andrew to go along the emergency lane on the side to help bypass the mess and reach exit 278 onto Old Dixie Highway. The agents reached the bank within an hour as they sidestepped traffic slowly, one traffic jam after another.

The group entered the bank as Agent Tim Horton got to the main counter, showed his identification, and asked for the manager. The clerk immediately went to the bank manager's office to notify the manager that there was an FBI agent that wanted to speak to him. Agent Horton didn't have to wait a long time. It seemed no sooner did the clerk enter the bank managers off that the manager followed by the clerk came to the counter to speak to Horton. The bank manager introduced himself as George Santos as he extended his hand. Agent Horton grabbed it and gave it a firm authoritarian handshake.

"I would like to speak to you in reference to the missing five thousand dollars and this client that opened a new account one day with the missing money going through his account the next morning." Stated Horton.

"Certainly, would you please come to my office so that we can discuss the incident in private." Responded the bank manager.

Horton nodded affirmatively and went behind the counter when the clerk unlocked and drew back the half-door to allow Horton to get in and he could follow the manager back into his office. The manager closed the door behind them.

AGENT ANDREW WENT TO the Sheriff's office which was located approximately less than a mile from the bank. Andrew showed his credentials and was immediately taken to the office of the deputy sheriff who was in charge. The deputy sheriff introduced himself as Billie Burns and asked how he could help the agent. Andrew quickly gave the deputy sheriff a breakdown of their investigation of not only the missing five thousand dollars from the bank but also the bank's client Shane O'Donovan. Billy explained that he had already formed a small task force to investigate not only the missing money but also to try and locate this Shane O'Donovan. So far they have not been able to find him yet. The address that was given turned out to be an empty building that had burnt down last year. We tried to contact the gentleman via the cell phone number that was given. But that was unsuccessful. The phone number was fictitious. He had an all point bulletin for this Shane O'Donovan if that was his name. The deputy sheriff had no doubt that if this guy O'Donovan was still in the area they would find them. Agent Andrew ask the deputy sheriff if had any description of this guy. He said he had. There was no way you couldn't spot him in a crowd. According to the assistant bank manager that opened the account said that this gentleman was around six feet six inches tall, around two-hundred and eighty pounds of muscle, and had a fiery red beard and long red hair to his shoulders. Agent Andrew agreed with the deputy that it would be very difficult not to spot this guy in a crowd. Andrew stood up and gave the deputy sheriff his card and asked him to please contact him if there were any updates on this character. Andrew left the station to go rejoin Horton who was at the Bank of America.

THE MANAGER COULDN'T understand how the client O'Donovan, if it was truly him had been able to remove the five thousand dollars from the bank via his account number in so little time. Horton agreed with the manager but explained that they were also investigating a person, male or female that was a skilled hacker that has created quite a mess with the authorities. Horton was sure that he had heard about it through the news and the media. The manager quickly understood the possible connection between the client Shane O'Donovan and this skilled hacker. If it was true that they had collaborated together to steal the five thousand dollars then it would have been quite easy for them to accomplish their goal. Agent Horton thanked the bank manager for his time and gave him his card while asking him to contact him immediately if he had any news on the missing money or Shane O'Donovan and left the office.

Agent Andrew was waiting for agent Horton as Horton came out of the bank manager's office. Andrew quickly informed Horton of what he found out at the sheriff's office. That the deputy sheriff had investigated the home address and phone number that was listed at the bank, and they found the information fictitious. He also described Shane O'Donovan was six feet six inches tall, around two-hundred and eighty pounds and full of muscle and had a fiery red beard and shoulder long hair. Agent Horton understood that they were trying to find a needle in a haystack but made a point that it wouldn't stop them. He felt sure that this guy or guys would make a mistake. They would trip up somewhere and he would be there to get them.

Chapter 9
Love is Grand

JUAN AND THE O'BRADYS were up at the crack of dawn, and they packed everything and were on the road before the sun was up. Within the hour they were back on interstate ninety-five crossing the bridge into the state of Georgia. Shane and Brian were in the back seat sleeping and snoring so loudly that it would wake the dead. Juan was looking at Shannon as she was looking out the passenger window. She didn't notice how Juan kept staring at her. Juan was starting to realize that he unexpectedly had fallen in love with this red-headed Irish beauty. Shannon turned towards Juan and caught him staring at her as she smiled. She knew that look. She had seen that look, many times from men that she wasn't interested even to talk to. But she felt different about Juan. She had never felt about any man like she felt about Juan. This was different. She wish that she could have some time with Juan without her father and brother 's piercing eyes. She had to find out if Juan felt the same way about her as she felt about him. It was driving her crazy!

Juan started to talk about anything as long as he could speak to her. Shannon asked Juan where they were heading. High Falls RV camp near Jackson, Georgia was the destination that Juan told Shannon. He stated that it was absolutely beautiful there. Shannon smiled and told Juan that she couldn't wait to see it. They continued with small-talk. Anyone could see that Juan was wooing Shannon.

One thing went unnoticed, Shannon's father was not sleeping. He was watching what was happening between his daughter and Juan. He was furious and he would have to do something about it. He would have to take out Juan when the time came. When Shane felt that Juan was no longer needed for his expertise as Hades.

"There is the sign for High Falls state park in five miles." Said Shannon.

"It a beautiful park with plenty of privacy, it's nice and hilly being in the mountains of Georgia, I guarantee that you will, not forget it." Expressed Juan.

"I'm sure, I won't" answered Shannon.

Juan was happy about that. He wasn't feeling well. He was feeling one of his migraines coming on and he hadn't had one in months. Juan kept quiet the last couple miles until they entered the state park and helped disconnect the camper from the truck. They quickly connected the water and electricity. The problem Juan saw was that this park didn't have an internet connection. He would have to use a hotspot which made it very easy for the authorities to triangulate their location. Juan knew It was too dangerous to use a hotspot. But he didn't have a choice. He had to attack again. He couldn't allow the authorities to catch their breath. He felt that he had the authorities stumbling, and he wanted them on their knees.

"Are you alright Juan?" asked Shannon.

"No, I'm not feeling very well. I'm starting to get one of my migraines, which I haven't had in months. I am going to go for a walk towards the lake, and try and get rid of it"

"Mind if I go with you?"

Juan smiled and said that would be very nice if she came along. Juan and Shannon started towards the lake as Shannon noticed her father's aggravation of her ignoring his wishes not to go with him. She didn't care. She wanted to be with Juan, and she refused to let her father tell her what she could do or not do and who she could see or not see. And far as she was concerned her decision was final. The lake was down the hill a little to the left of their site. It was a beautiful site to see. The water was very calm, it was like glass as the reflections of the tree line across the lake was perfectly clear. It was like looking at a photo. The temperature was nice and cool with a bit of cloudiness that presently covered the late afternoon sun. There was a shady area near the waterfront with a teak swinging porch style chair. Juan held onto the swing until Shannon sat down and then Juan sat down beside her. They sat there for an unknown period of time. Talking about their lives and experiences. Where they've been and where they would like to go back to. Nothing serious or life changing, just some pleasantries. Both checking each other out. As the time passed Juan felt more and more at ease and comfortable talking with Shannon. Little that he realize that she felt the same about him. Juan was slowly ever so slowly moving closer and closer to Shannon. She acted as if she didn't notice that he was coming closer to her, Shannon only kept smiling at Juan. Juan decided to make his move as his left arm wrapped around Shannon as he drew closer for a kiss, but...

"Hey guys, what are you doing? Supper is ready, come on, dad is getting angry." Yelled out Brian as he snickered away. He knew he interrupted Juan's move, but he was sure there would be more chances in the future.

Juan couldn't believe Brian's timing. He was so close to kissing Shannon he could actually taste her lips. He looked back at Shannon, and she smiled at him as she stood up. She knew she had to go right away. She had already got her father upset, there was no point pushing her luck. So, holding Juan's hand they went back to the camp site. The supper was already in large bowls on the picnic table next to the camper.

"The best meal in the world, Irish stew." Said Shane.

As Juan sat down beside Shannon, Brian brought out four cold bottles of Killian. And as soon his father sat down, Brian lifted his beer to give a toast to the beautiful and very missed, Ireland. Everyone lifted their beers and shouted, Ireland.

Shane was right, as far as Juan was concerned and he told Shane that, this Irish stew, and the cold Killian beer, were great and was definitely the best he has ever had. Shane smiled and lifted his beer towards Juan and thanked him for the compliment. Brian and his father were soon in a political conversation on how bad the English had treated the Irish. It turned into an argument not on whether the British had treated the Irish badly but on how badly the Irish were treated. While the argument ensued Shannon slowly let her hand lightly brush against the inside of Juan's thigh. Juan almost jumped out of his seat. He turned to look at Shannon to see a wide smile on her face. Juan was going crazy. He wanted so badly to embrace her. All that Juan was thinking was that he wished that her father and brother would disappear for a couple of hours. Brian came out with four more Killian beers for everyone. Juan thanked Brian even though he didn't want to have one. Brian did this four more times before Juan stated that he was getting a little buzzed so excused himself and went straight to bed.

Juan woke up a few hours later as he looked at his watch. It was one thirty a.m., and it was dark in the camper, and it was very quiet. Too quiet, thought Juan. He couldn't hear Shane snoring. Juan thought either Shane wasn't in the camper, or he was dead. He continued to lay in his cot as he could hear the sweet purring of Shannon as she slept. Juan decided to get up, making as little noise as possible. He slowly tip toe around the camper to see that both Shane and Brian were not there. He carefully opened the camper side door and went out. The truck was gone and so were Shane and Brian. Where did they go, Juan wondered? He wasn't sure, but he was definitely suspicious. He sat in one of the folding chairs and waited for the boys to get back from their little trip. Juan was scared of the security of the group if Shane and Brian did something stupid and got involved with the law. It was almost two hours before Juan saw the lights of the truck coming down the hill and heading towards their camp site. The truck stopped and the guys got out.

"Where, were you guys?" asked Juan.

"What, are you my mother?" said Brian.

Juan just tried to explain that he was apprehensive that they might have accidentally got involved with the law. That it would have totally blown their cover. They agreed and explained that they both felt that they needed to go for a drink, and they were lucky to find an Irish bar called the *4 Leaf Clover* a few miles north of the park. Juan couldn't believe how irresponsible these guys were.

"Okay, I'm going to sleep." Said Shane.

"Me also." Said Brian.

They got into the camper while Juan stayed in his chair. Juan sat there nodding his head in disbelief. What was he going to do with these morons? He decided to go back to bed and try and get some sleep. He was too tired to make any decisions tonight. He'll think about what he'll do tomorrow with some rest.

Tomorrow is another day.

IT WAS ALMOST NOON when I felt Shannon shaking my shoulder to wake me up.

"Time to wake up lazy bones."

Juan opened his eyes as he turned around and saw Shannon's beautiful face. He smiled at her as he took a huge stretch. He attempted to wake his body up. He sat up and saw Shannon place a cup of coffee for him on the counter. He thanked her and stood up to get his coffee and walked out of the camper and sat down on one of the folding chairs. He knew that he had fallen behind with his hacking, so he decided he would start as soon as he finished his coffee.

Juan only had one problem. That was to concentrate on hacking and not allow his mind to be overtaken by his passion for Shannon.

He wasn't convince of his ability to do so. but he would try. Juan finally finished his coffee, got up and went back into the camper. He sat in front of his laptop and like so many times he entered into his hacking software which he created. It didn't take long for his bold Red link to pop up. He sat back, and he felt a certain malicious form of pride, over the accomplishment of the chaos that he had caused. Then again there is always room for more, he believed, always room for more. He decided to attack the DOJ and the Democratic party again. He was going to use *Brute Force Attack* on the DOJ, and then once he is in, he'll send some sweet little bots to really screw up their system. It took him not more than twenty minutes to accomplish his vicious deed with the DOJ and started to laugh to himself before disconnected his connection to the DOJ so that he could turn his mind on Democrats. Yes, this had to be a good one. He wanted this to win the Nobel prize for hacking. Juan wanted so badly to get under the skin of the Democratic party that they would literally start jumping out windows, driving over the cliff and maybe something more picturesque like Hari-Kari. So, he finally made up his mind on sending them a Phishing spam. Yea, a nice group of Sextortion scam, I know they will love it. Juan disconnected his connection to the internet; he didn't want anybody to be able to track him down. Juan didn't want to take any chances; he would suggest to everyone that it was imperative that they leave first thing in the morning. There was no point for them taking any more chances than they needed to. Everyone agreed, so the next morning they packed up everything and were back on north interstate ninety-five.

Chapter 10
Not Again

HORTON WAS TALKING with one of his junior agent when agent Peter walked into the room. Horton saw Peter approach and noticed by the look on his face that he wasn't bringing any good news. Horton waited for the bad news that he was about to tell him. Peter started to give Horton the breakdown of attack on the DOJ and the group of Sextortion scam that was sent to everyone in the congress including the house speaker. Horton sat down with hand rubbing his forehead. At that moment, retirement definitely came to mind. Peter waited for the shock of his news to Horton to pass before he spoke to agent Horton. He told him that he had found that the signal came from around south Georgia. Peter expressed to Horton that he felt that hacker was heading northward.

His first suspicion was when they were notified by the Palmetto police that were investigating a break in a home during the evacuation order that had been issued near the old Piney Point fertilizer plant wastewater near the old reservoir. This was very close to where our experts estimated where the first hack attack originated from. Then there was an attack which they were pretty sure came out from somewhere in the Everglades. We had the area checked, to try and find our hacker without success. We didn't receive another attack from that area. But the next one we got we were better prepared for. We were able to estimate the origin of the attack from the east coast around the St Augustine area.

"Now we believe that the present attack was from Georgia." Said Peter.

"Do we have any concrete idea where this attack came from? "asked agent Horton.

Peter was told that that they were have a problem with the way the hacker was send the connection around the world and they were having a hard time pinpointing the origin of the signal. They were hoping to determine the precise location within a few hours. Agent Horton was frustrated to say the least. The information for him was taking much to long for his liking.

"This waiting for any concise information on this hacker location is driving me to drink."

Agent Peter understood his frustration because he knew that agent Horton was under a lot of pressure from Washington. Horton decided to call in all the agents back to the office. He told Peter that he felt they should head for Georgia and maybe they will get some information while they are on the way.

*****

IT WAS A MATTER OF minutes Agent Horton and his whole task force were on the road in two separate SUV. Agent Peter was driving the lead SUV with agent Horton and agent Anne while the second SUV had agent Andrew driving with agent Arianne, agent Jesse, and Susan. They were heading north on interstate ninety-five towards Georgia. They finally were crossing the bridge which separated the State of Florida and Georgia. Peter finally could see the large sign *Welcome To Georgia.*

"Do we know where we are going agent Andrew? "asked agent Jesse.

"Not yet, but one thing is for sure it has something to do with either this guy Shane O'Donovan or the hacker," answered Andrew.

They knew that only time would tell for sure. Suddenly, the radio came on as they heard agent Peter speaking quickly on the radio. Andrew was trying to pay attention but for some reason there was a lot of static interfering with the call.

"Repeat the message Peter." said agent Andrew

"We just got a call that they have possibly pinned down the hacker's location."

"Where?"

"At the High Falls state park. It's around ten minutes from here. We got to move quickly; we don't want this son of a bitch to get away again."

Andrew immediately put the emergency lights on as he tried to catch up with the lead car that must have been traveling at close to one hundred miles an hour. Andrew concentrated on going around one car after another trying to catch up to Agent Peter who was driving like his life depended on it. Andrew could hear his fellow agents preparing themselves for a possible gunfight. He looked over to the agents as they were starting to put on their bulletproof vests.

It took them less than ten minutes to get to their destination as they drove into the park. They stopped at the ranger station to find out if anyone had left the park. The young female ranger told them that she did not know because she had just got there. Horton got out and instructed the agent Peter and Andrew to block the road out of the park.

Agent Horton grabbed his bullet proof vest from the back of the SUV and put it on. The junior agents came to Horton and stood in front of him waiting for his instructions. They listened to him as he instructed them that these guys are very dangerous. If they needed to, take them down with extreme prejudice. The agents knew what needed to be done. Horton motioned the group to spread out and be very quiet and very cautious. We don't want any collateral damage. They all nodded, and they understood Horton's instructions. They slowly started to walk down the road that led into the main part of the park.

It seemed that the park was pretty empty. They had a few tents in the tent area which they ignored, and at least a dozen RV and campers. There was quite a group of people outside starting their breakfast and sitting drinking their coffees. No one noticed the agents moving in until a young girl spotted them and pointed them out to her mother. The mother squealed as she saw the group approaching with their guns out and prepared for battle. With the woman's scream the other camps were definitely taken by surprise as they all stood up, with parents grabbing their children and holding them close for protection. Horton raised his hand as he tried to calm the situation.

Within a few minutes the agents had verified everyone to make sure that they were who they said they were. No one who looked like Shane O'Donovan was here. All possible internet connections were verified and a complete breakdown of all the park residents was brought to Agent Horton's attention. The agents with their guns in their holsters and any rifle, shotguns were safely held as nonthreatening position. They slowly gathered around Agent Horton.

"Well, we either miss these guys again or they were never here." Expressed Horton.

Horton asked agent Anne and Susan to go back up to the ranger station and get the list of all campers that are here or were here last night when she left and drive the cars back down. They both nodded affirmatively, they grabbed the keys from Peter, and Andrew, and ran up the hill. Horton spoke with the junior agents to try and formulate a plan for their next move. Peter spoke up first, that they knew most likely that they were driving in a north to northwest direction. So why shouldn't they split up and drive on a different path to hopefully get to them? Before, he had a chance to answer agent Peter when he heard the cars coming down the hill. Horton didn't think that it was a good idea. He felt that maybe they were heading north or northwest. But then again they might be smart enough to get us off their trail, and to start to head back south or even west.

"Let's find a good hotel, and get some lunch, and wait if any more information come over for us to move on."

They drove out of the state park and headed north a couple miles until they saw a La Quinta Inn and Suites where they stopped, got out and entered the building. Horton took four suites, and everyone went to their designated rooms with the instructions to meet back in fifteen minutes in the dining room.

There they were, sitting around a large circular table with only lunch on their minds.

Chapter 11
I need Internet access

"SO, WHERE ARE WE GOING to go now?" asked Shannon.

"We are slowly heading for Canada. But first we going to Greensboro KOA Journey." answered Juan.

Juan continued to say that it was a very nice KOA, and it had a good fast internet system there. He told them that he feels that they had taken a big chance at the last state park when he was forced to use local hot spots. He said that it was too easy for the authorities, which by now is the FBI, to find the exact location of his computer.

Shannon asked Juan what made him think that the FBI were now on their trail? He explained that they've broken enough federal laws and we've crossed state lines, which definitely makes it a federal issue. Shannon was not happy about that. She glanced at her father, who didn't seem at all bothered by the possibility that the FBI was after them.

"What are we going to do? First it was Scotland yard, then Interpol, and now FBI? Didn't we all come to the U.S. to escape capture? The FBI is as good as Scotland Yard, if not better." Exclaim Shannon.

"Be quiet, woman." Shouted Shane.

Shannon became silent immediately after the way her father spoke to her. She knew better than to challenge his authority. Juan glanced over at Shannon and assured her that they were safe. That the FBI will never catch them as long as they keep moving and follow their simple rules of engagement with the FBI. Shannon smiled back at Juan. She knew that Juan couldn't understand what her father's true intentions were. She knew her father had some underlining plan to cause some kind of destruction, for in his mind it would be a blow for the IRA. Brian was sitting next to his father, quietly listening to the exchange between his sister Shannon and his father. Brian agreed with Shannon. He also understood the reason they had escaped to the U.S. was to start a new life. Maybe a little off a straight line, but definitely not like the life they were trying to escape. He knew his father; he was always an IRA fanatical follower. Whether he was doing something for the IRA which they wanted or not. His father didn't care. He felt he knew what the right thing was to do for Ireland.

"Hey there's a Walmart ahead. We'll stop there and get ourselves some supplies and supper for tonight." Said Juan.

Juan drove into the parking lot and parked in an area specifically for RV and campers. Everyone got out and Juan asked Shannon if she would like to come with him to see what we might need for the next few days. She nodded yes.

The real reason Juan wanted Shannon to come with him was to assure her that he would not let anything happen to her. He reached out and held her hand tightly as he leaned over and gave her a kiss as he placed his lips on her delicate, sensuous mouth. His kiss lasted too long for Shannon's liking, as she pushed him away. Being pushed away took Juan by surprise as Shannon quickly looked around to make sure that her father or brother were not around. She quickly grabbed Juan's hand as she explained her fears if her father had seen them. He would have been furious and might have done something stupid. He had an uncontrollable temper. She pleaded with Juan to understand. He said he did. But now he understood a little better the rules of Shane's game. They were not a team, not comrades in arms, or even close to being friends. Juan realized that the relationship between him and Shannon's father could be severed at any time.

They started to go up and down the food lanes as they chose some supplies that were deeply needed, like eggs, bacon, bread, coffee, and some sandwich meats. They also got a couple of boxes of fried chicken, coleslaw, and potato salad. Shannon also felt that they had to get approximately more important than food, she told Juan. Juan stopped in his tracks as he tried to imagine what she meant.

"Toilet paper." giggled Shannon.

Juan smiled and agreed with their need for toilet paper. Juan turned and saw Brian heading their way. He was speculative about what was taking so long. Juan articulated to Brian that he didn't realize that they had a time limit. Brian agreed that they didn't. It wasn't like anyone had a date to go to. Juan and Shannon agreed. Brian said the only reason he came in was to buy a carton of Marlboro for his father. Shannon said that she felt that Juan and she had gotten all the supplies that they would necessitate for now.

They left Walmart after they paid and were on the road within minutes. They stopped a little later, in a rest area along interstate ninety-five. They brought the fried chicken, coleslaw and the potato salad as Shannon got the paper plates, knives, and forks to the picnic table. While Brian brought the beer. It was an unusually amiable dinner as everyone grabbed their pieces of chicken, a spoonful of coleslaw, and potato salad. As they were finishing, Shane asked Juan if he had emphatic on the next hack that he was going to do. Juan had a few ideas about where he was going next with his hacking, but he still wasn't sure.

With the picnic table cleaned off and any leftover supplies placed in the fridge in the camper, everyone got into the truck and was on their way to the KOA near Greensboro. They were lucky that Juan had called ahead to reserve a spot for their camper. He was given a password so that the gate would open so that they would be able to enter the RV park. When they arrived, Juan drove up to the gate. He entered the code into the code box. The gate slowly opened as the group impatiently waited.

Juan drove to the lot sixty-nine, which happened to be in the back of the park. Juan park and once again everyone poured out as they started to organize the water and electric connections. While Juan took care of what he thought was a priority. The important internet connection to the port on the side of the camper he attached the internet wire into the ethernet port. He then entered the camper to make sure that the internet connection worked perfectly. He started the computer, and it started right away, which was unusual for his computer. But he was happy that it did. As he was checking his connection to his computer, Shannon walked in.

"Is everything alright Juan?"

"Yes, the computer and the connection is working perfectly."

"Great, would you like to go for a walk?"

"I love to Shannon. But what about your father and brother?"

"They just drove out to check out the area."

"But how are they going to get back into the park?"

"My father saw the code you plugged into the code box."

"I hope he got it right?"

"We'll find out. So how about the walk I suggested?

"Sounds great, let's go."

Shannon and Juan stepped out of the camper and started to walk towards the front of the park. Shannon slid her hand into Juan. Juan stopped and smiled as he leaned over to kiss Shannon. This time Shannon was eager to return the kiss with a passion that not only astounded him, but also excited Juan. He held her in an embrace that took her breath away. Their kiss was finished as Shannon looked into Juan's eyes. He smiled as he told her that he was in love with her. That he has been in love with her for a while except he was too reluctant to tell her. Shannon told Juan that she was in love with him as well. She placed her moist lips against Juan as they embraced what seemed to Juan like an eternity. Juan's head perked up as he heard a vehicle approaching.

"That might be your father and brother, Shannon."

Shannon nodded her head in agreement. They headed back to the camper. They hurried back and sat down on the folding that they had placed outside of the camper and waited. They didn't have to wait long. Brian drove up to the camper and parked. Juan and Shannon wondered where Shane was? He wasn't in the truck. Brian got out and rushed to the passenger side of the truck and opened the door. Juan and Shannon sat there, wondering what the hell was wrong with Brian.

"Help me." Said Brian.

Juan stood up and went over to the truck, when he saw Shane leaning over towards the side of the driver. His shirt was covered with blood as he heard the grunts of pain coming from Shane's mouth.

"What the hell happened?"

"He was shot."

Brian explained that he was shot by a cashier at this liquor store when they tried to rob the place. Shannon moved in quickly to help them to get their father into the camper. The boys placed Shane on the couch as Shannon grabbed the side of her father and asked Juan to help her so she could examine his back. Juan lifted Shane onto his side as Shannon tore his shirt and wiped away the blood.

"Thank God the bullet went through. It didn't hit any major organs."

"Didn't hit any major organs. What the hell are you talking about, Shannon? Your father has been shot."

She said she knows. This has happened in the past in Ireland when the British were looking for him and her brother Brian. Juan was telling her that they needed a doctor for him, but Shannon once again explained to him that this had happened regularly back home, and she knew how to take care of a gunshot wound. Juan was not only in shock, because he had never seen anyone shot, especially someone he knew. But he was astonished at the calmness and authoritative ability of Shannon while he sat totally dumbfounded. All that he could do was to stare at the woman that he had fallen in love with, taking care of her father's gunshot wound.

While Shannon was taking care of her father, her brother Brian was outside working hard on cleaning blood stains inside the truck. It was a long and exhausting night for everyone. Especially for Shannon, who never left her father's side. Luckily, Shane had passed out from the pain. Juan was worried that somebody would hear his screams during the night.

The sun was slowly coming up over the horizon as Juan was sitting outside with what seemed to be his second pot of coffee. Luckily, a few of the RV's and campers were leaving early to get on the road heading to their next destination. The camper door opened as Shannon came out with a large mug of coffee. She sat down beside him as the new morning sun shone on her face, that made her blue eyes glitter like polished sapphires.

"You must be tired, my darling?"

"I am Juan. My father seem to be doing better. I'm afraid that he will live to do this again."

Juan questioned her if she knew why her father would go and rob a liquor store while they were all trying to live in Cognito? All she could answer was that was the way her father was. Every so often, he would become very bored, and he would get a graving for action. Juan answered that her father must be happy now. He got his action and almost got himself killed. Juan asked her, "do you think he would be able to travel?" She said no, he wouldn't be for a couple of days. With the conditions of the roads, he might tear open his wound and start bleeding again. Juan understood, but he wasn't happy about it. He would have to postpone any hacking tonight. He couldn't afford to take a chance on being pinpointed, since they were now unable to leave the park for a couple of days.

Chapter 12
Where the Hell are They

IN THE ROOM SEATED were eight exhausted agents from the FBI. It had been a grueling forty-eight hours. No one spoke, they just seemed to sit there with heads hanging low, while others were held up by the palm of their hand. They all wanted to escape from this place and run away to their bedroom to get a much needed, and much deserved rest. But it wasn't going to happen. Agent Horton walked into the room screaming.

"Wake up guys, there was a bombing at the White House gate. We've been called in to help."

Everyone jumped out of their seats as their adrenaline kicked in.

"Is there any indication of who or whom did this?" asked Andrew.

Agent Horton said that they had no idea who could have attempted to bomb the White House. The only information that he had was that at first it was thought it was a suicide bomber that brought the rental van to explode it, and cause as much damage that he could. After checking what was left of the van, they found no body parts.

"What do you mean, no body parts?" asked Agent Peter, as he was putting on his bulletproof vest.

Agent Horton explained to his junior agents that they found some form of an automatic system that drove the van remotely. They were scanning the whole area for clues or some form of information that would help them to figure out who the hell did this. So, they are calling all agents within a couple of hundred miles to aid with the investigation.

They got into the two Black SUV's again, and we're on the road with their lights flashing and sirens blaring as agent Andrew had called ahead to the highway police to open the path to help them to reach Washington without delay. The two black SUVs were speeding down the interstate as they approached numerous openings of traffic that were quickly opened by the highway police. Soon numerous highway police with their lights flashing and their sirens blaring were ahead of the two SUVs as they continued to clear the path for Horton and his agents.

Horton and his agents approached the White House when they were forced to stop and show their identification at numerous blockades. The authorities where not taking any chances on who or what was to be permitted near the white house. When the SUVs reached approximately a block from the White House they were forced to get out and walk the rest of the way. As they approached the scene of the explosion, Agent Horton recognized Agent Turner, who was in charge of cleaning up the chaos that had been created by an unknown perpetrator.

Agent Turner saw Horton coming to him as he held out his hand.

"Well, Agent Horton, how is going at your end of the table?"

"Not good. As a matter of fact, the table is as bare as it can be."

Horton brought Agent Turner up to speed on the investigation of the Hades Hacker. That they had found themselves at a standstill. Hades had been quiet for almost three days, and Horton had no idea what was happening and why the hacker had gone underground. But he was sure that he would come out of hiding soon.

"Do you think this could have been done by your hacker?" asked Agent Turner.

"I don't believe that he did this. It's not his forte. His specialty is to undermine our infrastructure."

Agent Turner changed the subject as he brought Horton up to date with what was happening there. He had every security camera checked to try to trace the path of the rental van and see if they could discover some images of our perpetrators. He asked Horton if he could head the verification of the security videos as he was stuck out here trying to organize this confusion. Horton said that he was glad to do that. He and his agents would check every video and let him know the moment they find anything.

Horton turned around and instructed the group to head towards the FBI headquarters. There they were to look at and catalog all the security videos that the FBI had. Hopefully, they would be able to see in the security videos anyone responsible for the van in question.

The White House was less than a mile from the FBI headquarters as the agent quickly reached the building, went up to the fourth floor, and entered the room where the videos were kept. They immediately started to view and catalog all the videos. They did not find any information about the perpetrators. All they were finding were videos of the truck heading towards the White House. Suddenly, agent Susan screamed.

"I got something, I got something here."

Agent Horton rushed to the table and sat next to agent Susan to view the video. He looked at the video a few times, trying to evaluate every possible clue that he could. He could see that there were two men. It was hard to recognize any distinct appearance that might help them to find these two men. Horton knew that he had to have some of the FBI experts, on enlarging, and enhancing the videos for possible more clues. So, he told her to bring the video upstairs so the video can be worked on. Horton also told agent Andrew to bring Agent Turner up to date with their findings. Andrew left immediately to find Agent Turner. Agent Horton instructed the other agents to continue viewing the videos hoping they would find more clues. One thing was for sure, that the two men that were on the video, did not fit the description of being a huge muscular man he was looking for.

SHANNON WAS ATTENDING to her father in the back bedroom and was trying very hard to make him as comfortable as it was possible to do. While in the other room, in front of their television, her brother Brian and Juan were busy watching a local news station. The news broadcaster was trying to explain what the up-to-date findings were, on the terrorist attack against the White House.

"I just hope they don't blame us for this, Brian." said Juan.

Chapter 13
We Better Stay Quiet

JUAN AND BRIAN CONTINUED to watch the news broadcaster explain what had happened and what the authorities led by the FBI were actively trying to resolve. Juan looked at Brian with a look of aggravation at what happened.

"Well, Brian, I've decided that we better stay quiet. We'll be here for a while, I think."

Brian nodded in agreement with Juan. They had to stay out of the limelight until things had a chance to quiet down. Anyway, both Brian and Juan knew that Shane needed as much time as they could give him to recuperate. Shannon came out of the room and got herself a cup of coffee while she asked if anyone wanted her to warm up their coffee. They both said yes please. As Shannon came over to refill their cups, Juan asked how was her father's condition? She said her father was vastly improved, and he should be able to travel by the weekend. That was the good news that Juan was interested in hearing. He was getting very nervous about being stuck in one spot without a backup plan to escape if he needed to. Juan got up to help Shannon with the cleaning of the breakfast dishes. While they were doing the dishes, Shannon started to speak very low as Juan struggled to hear her.

"Juan, you have to be careful. I am worried that my father has an underlying plan to create some kind of a catastrophic event in the United States."

"What makes you think your father is up to something?"

"Because I'm used to my father's perverted way of looking at things."

"What do you mean perverted?"

Shannon explained that her father saw the world in one way, and in one way only. He wants the total destruction of how the world is and how it sees itself. He is especially fanatical about the IRA. He wants the IRA to bomb everywhere. Not only in Great Britain, but throughout the world that he senses that they do not agree with his viewpoint.

"So why did he connect with me, back in Palmetto, Florida.?"

"He is using you as a steppingstone to an end. I'm not totally sure what that end is but I'm pretty sure once he no longer needs your services he'll get rid of you."

"Get rid of me. How?"

"That is the million dollar question, Juan. That is the question."

Juan continued to help Shannon with the cleaning, as his mind was overrun with thoughts of Shane's plans for him. Wherever his thoughts went, none ended well for him. They went from bad to worst. Juan felt that maybe it would be time for him to split up with the O'Brady clan. But Juan didn't like that idea because it meant he would lose Shannon. That was unacceptable. He just would have to be very careful and not trust Shane in any way.

Juan finished helping Shannon as she went back to the bedroom to check on her father. Juan went and sat down next to Brian, who was still listening to a newscaster talking about the bombing at the White House.

"Hey Brian, you have some guns, don't you?"

"Yea, why?

"Well, it starting to get a little crazy and I been feeling that I need some way to defend myself. Do you by any chance have an extra gun you could lend me?"

"Yea sure, I've got a Glock 17. I could lend it to you. Plus, a couple of clips."

"That would be great, Brian. That would surely ease my mind a bit."

Juan sat back as his mind had a sense of ease, and that he was in more control of his safety, after what Shannon had explained to him of her fears for Juan's safety through her father's hatred. He sat there and continued to talk to Brian as he laid out his plan. As soon as Shane was capable to start heading to Michigan to a beautiful, mostly deserted state park to stay. Juan felt that it would be a safe place for him to do a couple of hackings of the nation's infrastructure. Juan's only concern as he burst out laughing was that the state was in such disarray that the authorities wouldn't even notice that he created a huge mess.

Shannon came out of the back bedroom, as she walked over to the couch, to let them know that her father was feeling much better and was now resting. She asked Juan if he would like to accompany her. She stated that it was a beautiful day for a walk. Juan stood up and casually said that it was a good idea. He needed to get out of the camper, because he was starting to get a little stir crazy. Shannon opened the camper door as both Juan and Shannon stepped outside. As the door closed, Brian looked back towards the camper door and smiled. He understood what was going on with Juan and his sister, and he approved. Brian liked Juan and he felt that he would be a fine brother-in-law and if he didn't take care of Shannon, he'd kill him.

Chapter 14
Red Headed Brigand

AGENT HORTON WAS IN his office drinking a cup of crude oil that was passed as coffee when agent Andrew knocked on his office door, and Horton motioned him to come in.

"What can I do for you, Andrew?"

"I know this sounds crazy, but it's too big of a coincidence."

"What coincidence are you talking about?"

"Reading some reports that were coming over the wire, I saw something very interesting."

"Yea, what was that?" asked Horton.

"The day we were expecting Hades to do another one of his hacking and none came."

"Okay, what about it?"

"Well, in the suburbs of Greensboro, North Carolina, a seven-eleven store was robbed by a giant of a man, muscular, with long red hair to his shoulders, and a long red beard."

Agent Horton sat up in his chair. Andrew had his full attention now. As Andrew had said, what were the odds that such a big coincidence would pop up? Andrew continued to tell Horton that according to the police report that the cashier at the seven-eleven was carrying a gun under the counter.

"This guy from India who was the owner of the seven-eleven has been rob so many times, that he was fed up with it, so he bought himself a gun, and he shot the guy, and he was positive that he hit the assailant. So, I investigated all the hospitals in the area and, like the police report, stated that no one has been admitted with a gunshot wound the last few days."

"So, he's either dead or hiding somewhere that is low profile and mainly migrants, and nobody knows or care who their neighbors are."

"Like maybe a trailer or RV park?" said Andrew.

Horton nodded unquestionably, yes. He told Andrew to get the rest of the agents and to meet in the conference room within thirty minutes. Andrew left right away as he was ordered to. As instructed, the agents were in the conference room waiting patiently for Agent Horton. Horton came into the room and discussed his plan to get this hacker. First, they were to break up in four pairs with the back of local police and go to every trailer park in the area that Horton showed in the park around Greensboro, North Carolina. He pointed out the station in Greensboro, which will be their operation center. He checked and double checked that all the junior agents knew exactly what was expected of them.

"We are looking for Shane O'Donovan who is an Irish man with this description, muscular, with long red hair to his shoulders, and a long red beard. This man is considered dangerous and most likely violent. Do not underestimate this man. He is wanted for terrorism, among other personal attributes, by Interpol and Scotland Yard."

A few of them glanced at the agent beside them with a look of amazement. They were excited about going after a big number. They were all biting at the bit. They all were listening to Agent Horton attentively. They wanted to make sure that they didn't miss any piece of information.

"Alright, everyone knows where they are going?" Asked Horton.

They all nodded that they were.

"Alright, let's get going and I want everyone to report every thirty minutes. Okay, let's go."

The group got into their vehicles after they loaded it up with all the necessary equipment and headed to their designated destinations.

BRIAN, JUAN, AND SHANNON were outside the camper talking about Shane when the camper door flew open with a bang when it hit the side of the camper. All three were startled by the noise.

"So, what the hell are we still here for? Do I have to make all the decisions?"

Juan, Shannon, and Brian stood there looking at each other amazed that Shane was standing in front of them yelling. Shane kept yelling that we had to get out of here and head for our next spot. Everyone agreed as they scurried around, preparing to leave.

They were out of the campground within the hour. Juan once again was at the wheel. He knew that his next destination was in Michigan. It would be a long drive for them before they got there. Juan was hungry, and he was happy that Shannon always made sure there were an adequate amount of sandwiches for everyone. Juan started on his first toasted tomato with a miracle whip sandwich when he asked Shannon to pass him a soft drink. Shannon lifted the cooler cover to grab Juan a cola and passed it over to him. Juan thanked her as he was watching her in his mirror. He could see Shane laying there with his eyes closed. As far as he was concerned, Shane didn't look good. Not looking good at all. They should have stayed another day to give Shane a chance to recuperate for a bit longer. Could of, should of, hind-site is 20 20 and it's too late to do anything about it now. Shannon was praying that Shane's stitches would hold or he would risk having the wound bleed again.

AGENT HORTON RECEIVED his fourth call from his agents. None of them had any great news. He told them all to continue to their next designated location, and to continue to report back every half hour. Horton sat down and grabbed his cup of steaming hot coffee and brought it to his lips as he slowly sipped it. The synapses of his mind were exploding at warp speed. He knew that he was right on their trail. But he seems to always be a few steps behind.

"Why the hell is this son of a bitch not doing something so we can figure out where he is?" screamed Horton.

His frustration was starting to drive him crazy. This guy had to make a mistake, any mistake, so they could find him. He decided that he needed to go out for a walk anywhere. As long as it was outside of the building. Horton opened the door and was preparing to walk out when his phone rang. It was agent Andrew. He had just finished checking out the Greensboro KOA Journey at 1896 Trox street off interstate forty. He spoke with the Ranger here, and he told me that a camper who was paid up for two more days left a couple hours ago, going east towards interstate eight forty. Horton was ecstatic with what he's been waiting all day to hear. Horton told Andrew to wait there, he would notify the rest of the team to meet him, and he would take a chopper, and get there as quickly as the chopper could get him there.

JUAN WAS RUBBING HIS eyes. He was getting tired. They were near Roanoke, Virginia. There they could find a Cracker Barrel at exit 150. Where they could stay overnight in their parking lot. Shannon asked if Cracker Barrel was not a restaurant. Juan agreed that it was, but most Cracker Barrel restaurants allowed a certain amount of campers to stay overnight without a charge, so Juan told them that was where they were going to spend the night. Plus, they were going to have supper there, his treat. Juan said that he loved their catfish dinner.

They drove into the parking lot and parked at the first space allotted to campers. Juan was surprised that there were no other campers there yet. They slowly got out, making sure that Shane was doing okay. He nodded yes, so they walked into the restaurant and waited for a hostess to welcome them to Cracker Barrel and bring them to their seats and gave everyone a menu. She told them that their waitress would be there in a moment to get their orders. Small talk ensued as the O'Bradys discussed the menu, with Juan offering some recommendations. He suggested their fried chicken dinner, which was great and also their steak dinner was also one of his favorites. A few minutes later, a very personable waitress with an amazing smile came up to the table, and took their orders, and asked what they would like for a drink. Everyone took some water except for Brian and his father; they had a beer. Shannon decided to have a glass of red wine. Juan said that having a glass of wine was a great idea.

As Juan was finishing his catfish dinner that he loved, he looked across to Shane and his son, who were finishing their fourth glass of beer. Juan thought that Shane most likely would feel no pain tonight, and hopefully get a good night's sleep.

They were back in the camper and were sitting down talking about soccer in Great Britain. Juan had no idea about soccer in Europe, never mind about England.

"Manchester is number one team in England." Said Brian.

"I personally like Liverpool." said Shannon.

"Liverpool might have been good for the Beatles, but not for soccer." said Brian.

Shannon made a face to her brother that made Juan believe that it looked like she felt he was full of baloney. Juan just sat there with no intentions of getting in between Shannon and her brother Brian over British soccer. He didn't feel that it was much of a sport. Now, let's take hockey. Now that was a man's sport. Juan wanted to talk about it, but no one was interested in, or even understood, the game that was the most violent game since the gladiators of ancient Rome.

"Really?" said Juan.

They decided to get some shuteye, because they would be leaving first thing in the morning, so they could get to Strait's state park in St Ignace, Michigan, by nightfall.

The sun was coming up above the horizon when their truck with the camper left the Cracker Barrel parking lot.

"How long will it take us approximately, Juan, to get to Michigan?" asked Shannon.

"It's around eight hundred miles and approximately twelve hours to get there. Why?"

"Just wondering."

"Why don't you try to get some sleep? You haven't had a chance to get a good night's sleep since your father was shot."

Shannon agreed and pushed the seat back and closed her eyes.

Chapter 15
Finally, Strait Mackinac

THEY FINALLY ARRIVED at St Ignace state park. Brian suggested that they go into town to any local restaurant for supper. Everyone agreed. They stopped at a pizzeria. It was well known for their Italian pizza with chicken, and bacon, and bread sticks. Brian asked the server to bring them a pitcher of beer and not let it run out. The server said okay, but then asked them what type of pizza they wanted. They agreed to get the extra-large house specialty.

The supper was great, and everyone was very impressed with the service. Brian paid the bill, and they walked out. It didn't take them long to get back to the camper. They entered the camper as Brian opened the television to check to see if there was anything interesting on the news. The broadcaster was talking about everything except what Brian and Juan wanted to hear. They both sat there with disappointed looks on their faces.

"What are you going to do now, Juan? It looks like they've forgotten about Hades."

"I think you're right, Brian. I got to remind them of Hades. I'll start that right now."

Juan went to his backpack and removed his computer. He sat on the couch and started his computer up. He took off his baseball cap and placed it on the counter.

Shannon looked at Juan's face and saw a face of determination with a purpose. For the first time, Juan didn't look at Shannon. As a matter of fact, he didn't even notice her. His face and mind were deep in the computer. His eyes didn't seem to even blink. He seemed possessed and was a man on a mission to cause as much of chaos as he could.

"Juan are you alright?" asked Shannon.

Juan never took his eyes off the computer, and he never answered Shannon. Shannon looked at her brother, he only shook his head. Not totally understanding what was going on, Brian just shrugged. Shane came into the room from the back of the camper.

"What's going on?" asked Shane.

"Juan is possessed. I think he's starting to hack again." Said Brian.

Shane was ecstatic that Juan was back on his crusade to destroy the United States. He told Brian that they needed to go out for a drink. Brian was all for it. They told Shannon that they would be home late and for her not to bother to wait for them.

Brian and Shane stepped out of the camper, got into their truck, and drove away.

Shannon watched her father and brother drive away and shut the door. She turned around and looked at Juan, typing up a storm of unknown terms and symbols that Shannon didn't understand. She didn't bother to talk to Juan, who seemed to be lost in his hacking surreal world. Nothing around him mattered.

Shannon filled her cup of coffee and decided to go outside to drink it. As she sat there, she could hear the rumbling of a storm coming. She had heard that some of the storms over the great lakes were usually storms to never forget. As she sat there, watching the lightening, light up the sky announcing the oncoming storm.

THE IRISH BAR WAS PACKED as usual with students from the local college. Bill O'Reilly the bartender, was rushing around serving customers at the bar and filling out the waitress's orders. Bill knew he could see that it was going to be another one of those crazy nights. Since the college had won its opening basketball game from their main competitor a private Catholic school. The noise in the bar was getting louder and louder as Bill was desperately trying to hear the orders that were being thrown at him. All that Bill was hoping for was not another competitor's bar brawl. He was alone, and if a fight ensued, it would not be a pretty night for him. The last time there was a brawl in the bar, he ended up with twenty-two stitches on the side of his head, and a hell of a concussion that still hurt him each time he thought of it.

He then heard a scream that this was the worst service in town, and he sucked as a bartender. That was it. He was not going to tolerate these insults tonight; he was going to throw this bum out. He went to where he felt the insults were coming from when grabbed the client by the back of his collar as the guy screamed.

"Whoa, whoa baby brother."

Bill lowered his arm as a smile came across his face. He was happy to see his brother. It's been a while since he saw him. He knew that his older brother, Sean, was always too busy for them to get together.

"How are you doing, Sean?"

"Doing pretty good, and you?"

"Running around like a chicken with its head cut off."

"Well, that is pretty normal for you, isn't it? As Sean snickered.

"Very funny. No wonder there is so much crime around here. Policemen like yourself are always in bars trying to get a free beer."

"Now that you mention it, get me a Killian, will you?"

Bill smiled at his brother as he stooped to the cooler and got a Killian for Sean. He hardly had time to open the beer and give it to his brother when customers were yelling for another drink and waitresses waiting for their orders to be filled.

Sean turned around as he leaned against the bar as he glanced around. His eyes fell onto an absolutely beautiful student with long blond hair that was staring at him. Sean smiled, and the student walked towards him and introduced herself.

"Hi, my name is Bobbi-joe. What's yours?

"Sean O'Reilly."

"Well, Sean O'Reilly I have a nice big joint in my purse. Why don't we go outside and get more acquainted?"

"You see, my darling, it's my night off. Because usually I would arrest you if I was at work, a police officer on duty."

The beautiful student's eyes opened wide as she knew that she had made a big mistake offering Sean a share of her joint. Sean bent over and whispered into the young student's ear. She looked into his eyes, smiled, and turned around and disappeared into the crowd.

Sean leaned back against the bar again as he cursed the fact that he was a cop. He would have loved to get to know Bobbi-joe better. Oh well, she was too young for him, anyway. When the evening ended, Sean and Bobbi-joe would have nothing to talk about. He knew that they had absolutely nothing in common. He turned around and motioned to his brother for another beer. While he was waiting for the beer, he was looking toward the large mirror on the wall behind Bill. He had a great observation of the crowd behind him and the stairway that led to the entrance of the bar. It sure was a busy night. The bar was at capacity as he tried to get an approximation of how many people were here. He gave up, he decided that the bar was just crammed in solid and left it at that.

He finished his third beer as his brother delivered his fourth one. He started to sip on the beer as his eyes returned to the mirror and observed as a group of students were entering the bar. He continued to look at all the people entering, as he knew that the crowd had passed the legitimately allowable capacity for the place. Sean suddenly perked up as he saw two men entering the bar, the first one was a big man, over six feet tall, two hundred and fifty pounds with fiery red shoulder length hair and a long red beard. The second man was a lot smaller, also a redhead, but his hair was short, and he was well shaven. He remembered the notice of an all point bulletin from the FBI for two men. One a muscular guy over two hundred pounds, solid built with a fiery red hair and beard. Sean couldn't believe that this could be the same men. He watched them carefully as the men intermingled with the crowd and ordered some Killian beers. Sean watched the two men like a hawk. There was no way that he was going to let them out of his sight. He didn't dare go out to call for backup. He might lose them, and it was much too noisy to try to call for backup here. He was stuck waiting for them to leave so he could follow.

It was getting late, and the bar was going to close soon, even though the place was still pretty busy. Sean had to change to coke, or he would have been in his normal condition when he visited his brother, a level of drunkenness. Where he would end up, sleeping on his baby brother's couch.

Finally, the short redheaded guy stood up as he was talking to the bigger guy who finally stood up and stumbled over his chair, where he quickly recovered his balance. Sean realized that the man was looking straight at him, but then he turned towards his friend. They spoke for a few moments as the short-haired guy turned around and headed towards and went up the stairs as he left the bar with the big muscular guy following right behind him.

Sean waited a few moments before he climbed the stairs and stood against the doorway. He saw the short-haired guy get into the truck as he started it. Sean quickly scurried to his car, started it, and waited for the truck to move. Suddenly, he noticed something coming to the side of his car. Before he had a chance to react three shots were fired as the driver's side window exploded. The bullets hit Sean as he tried to duck out of the line of fire. Sean crumpled to his side as his life slowly drained out of his body. A moment later, Sean O'Reilly was dead.

THE PARKING LOT WAS full of flashing lights as an officer stood talking to Bill O'Reilly about his brother. He couldn't believe that his brother was dead. Shot dead by some low life assassin who never gave him a chance. His brother's gun was still in his holster. The officer was desperately trying to get his attention, but Bill could only think of his brother being gone forever. He would never get the chance to irritate and tease his big brother ever again. Bill couldn't help himself; he covered his face as he burst out crying. The officer decided to give him some space. There was no point trying to talk to him in his present condition. The officer decided that he would be more productive, so he moved on to interrogate some of the customers from the bar.

Bill was still trying to get his emotions under control as he wiped the tears off his face with his shirtsleeve. Detective Ed Johnson, an experienced detective of the small Ignace police force, approached him. Bill immediately recognized the detective as a good friend of his brother and who had accompanied him multiple times to the bar. The detective sat beside Bill and offered his deepest condolences.

"Your brother and I have been friends for a long time, as you know. I had just started as a rookie detective when your brother graduated from the police academy at the head of his class. He will be sorely missed, and I promise you, Bill, I will find the guy that killed him."

Detective Johnson asked Bill if he knew or had any ideas who the culprit or culprits could have been that killed his brother. He said that he didn't know who had it out for him. He was well known and liked here at the bar.

"Hey, wait a minute, now that I think about it, my brother was very interested in two men

that had come to the bar."

"Do you recall what they looked like?"

"Well, these guys would be hard to forget. There were two men. The older man was a huge dude. He was definitely over six feet and around two hundred and fifty pounds. He had long shoulder length red hair and a bright red beard. While his buddy was also a redhead but much smaller, with no beard and short hair. Now that I think about it, I saw my brother leave when the two guys had left. "

"Are you absolutely sure of this description of the two guys that were here?"

Bill nodded affirmatively. Like he had told the detective that he would never forget them. Especially the big man.

Detective Johnson sat there for a couple of minutes wondering if this was a coincidence that these two guys fit perfectly with the APB he read earlier today from the FBI. He decided coincident or not he was going to notify the FBI about what happened here today. Let them figure out if his suspicions are valid or not.

Detective Johnson got back to the station after he documented all the evidence of the assassination of his friend Sean O'Reilly. He sat as he listened to the rings on his call to FBI headquarters in Washington, DC. Eventually, the call was answered.

"FBI, agent Gonzales speaking."

Detective Johnson introduced himself and explained the reason for his call. The agent asked for his number and that Special Agent Horton was in charge of the case. She stated that she would relay this information to Agent Horton, and he would call back shortly. Johnson thanked the FBI agent and terminated the call. Johnson sat at his desk wondered if this FBI agent would ever call him back. Whether he would or not he had made a promise to Bill that he would find his brother's killer. He got up from his desk and went to pour himself a cup of coffee. He first fill his coffee cup almost one quarter full with sugar. He knew the coffee would be burned and it would taste rancid. He needed something to cover it up so that it could at least be drinkable.

As Johnson sat at his desk drinking the sweet, rancid concoction that he had created, his smart phone rang. Johnson answered his phone as he introduced himself to the caller and heard the voice on the phone state that he was Agent Horton from the FBI returning his call.

Johnson was surprised that the FBI agent had called him back so quickly.

"You left me a message that one of your officer was killed by possibly two men. Are you able to give me some information about what happened?"

Detective explained to him that Sean O'Reilly was ambushed, shot, and killed while he was sitting in his car. The detective said that the victim's brother, who was the bartender at the bar stated that he noticed that his brother, who normally drinks a lot of beer, at one point stopped. He had started eyeing these two men and eventually followed them out of the bar. According to Bill O'Reilly one of the men was a well-built giant of a man. Over six feet tall and over two hundred pounds with shoulder length red hair and a fiery red beard and his partner was a smaller guy also red headed but short and he had no beard.

Anyway, the detective explained that in less than ten minutes, the officer was shot three times, which killed him.

"Do you have clues on where these guys are?

"Not yet, we are trying to make out which state license was on the car. I know it wasn't a Michigan license plate. Possibly a Florida plate, but I'm not positive."

"How about the vehicle that was used to for them to get away with? What kind of vehicle was it.?"

"A truck."

"A truck, heh."

"Yes, I should have more concise information of the truck in question in a couple of hours."

"Excellent, that would help."

"We are working on it, and I should be able to bring you up to date as soon as we find out."

"Listen, I'm organizing my staff and we'll be flying there tomorrow morning."

"Great, looking forward to meeting you agent Horton."

Chapter 16
The Calvary has Arrived

The corporate jet approached the airport as it slowly came down, landed, and taxied to the hangar where a half dozen officers with detective Johnson were waiting. Agent Horton got off the plane with his junior agents following him. Detective Johnson approached and shook Horton's hand, welcoming him and his junior agents to St Ignace.

As they all were heading to the St Ignace police station, Detective Johnson gave Agent Horton an up-to-date report on what they had discovered since yesterday. The group arrived at the station as everyone entered the station and were directed straight to the conference room. Everyone sat down after they got themselves some fresh coffee.

"So, Detective, what have you been able to find out?"

"We were able to find that the truck that was in the video was a black Expedition Platinum MAX SUV with the Florida license plate from SU-E359."

"Have you been able to find the truck in question?" asked Horton.

"No, not yet, but I have an all-points bulletin on the truck. We haven't got anything yet."

Horton sat there, a little disappointed in the results of tracking the truck. So, he turned to the desk and started to talk with the group as he broke down the duties and breakdown of the area that each group was responsible for.

"Have you had a chance to go to any of these trailer parks?"

"No, Agent Horton, we haven't yet?" said detective Johnson.

"I think we need to go check it out right now."

"Right." Said Johnson.

"Jesse and Anne, I want you two to get to this trailer park that seems to be near here to see if you can find that truck."

"Okay, we will go there right away." said Jesse with Anne nodding in agreement.

Agents Jesse and Anne left the room and headed to the garage, where they were given one of their courtesy cars to use. They ask one of the patrolmen the direction of the park. They were given the instructions that seemed pretty easy. They drove out of the garage, turned right until they reached the main street, where they turned right again.

It didn't take them long to get to the park as they drove in and stopped at the ranger station to speak to the woman that was receiving the park guests. The agents got out of their car and entered the station. Agent Jesse introduce themselves to the woman and explained why they were there. Agent Anne described the vehicle in question, but the lady didn't know. She stated that she's been off the last few days, so she wasn't sure if the vehicle was there. Jesse told her that he and Anne would go and verify if the car was in the park. The agents thank the woman for her help and drove into the park to look at the campers. It was a beautiful park with not much privacy, as they were able to see a large area without trouble. They slowly drove around the park with no luck. There were no vehicles that fit the description of the car in question. They stopped at the ranger station again to see if there were any other parks in the area. The attendant told them that there was one around ten miles away that was situated right along Lake Michigan. Jesse asked for instructions on how to get to the park. The attendant came around the corner and went to the stand which held a lot of sightseeing pamphlets. She pulled one out and showed it to the agents. She returned behind the counter so she could grab her yellow highlighter from the drawer of her desk and marked the route while explaining how they could get there from the park. The agents thank the woman for her help and drove away towards the second park.

Chapter 17
They Never Saw it Coming

AGENT JESSE AND ANNE arrived at the second park where they drove in and stopped at the ranger station. There was a sign on the window that said that the ranger or attendant was gone for the day. Jesse looked at Anne as he commented that it was a great job to be finished already. It was only two o'clock in the afternoon. They continued into the park as they parked at a designated overflow parking lot. Both Jesse and Anne stepped out of the car as they saw that this park was packed with campers and in one section tents. They knew that it would take them a long time to be able to go through all the sites. Jesse gave an enormous sigh as they approached the first camper. While approaching, they were looking in every direction for a chance to see the car they were looking for. They didn't see it, but they were still checking each camper in case they had exchanged it for another vehicle. The campers that received them were pleasant, yet no one had any information about the were about of a Ford Black Expedition. Jesse and Anne were getting a little frustrated by the chance that they would find this dam ford. They approached a turn in the road as they looked to an area that was surrounded by trees. Jesse glanced at Anne as he pointed out the car that hid in the shade of the big oak tree. A big smile came across Anne's face. At last, they hoped that found the right Black Ford Expedition. Both Jesse and Anne had not noticed eyes that had been staring at them as they went from camper to camper. Especially when the man and woman stopped and pointed to their camper.

"There is only one way to find out if that's the right black Ford Expedition." Said Anne.

"Your right Anne. I'll go to the door. You stay behind me and back me up."

"Okay but be careful. They're considered very dangerous."

The agents slowly approached the camper as Anne stayed back with her hand on her service revolver, just in case, as Jesse got to the door and knocked. No one answered, so Jesse knocked again. The door opened as Jesse looked at this huge sight of a man with red shoulder length hair and a fiery red beard.

"Can I help you?"

"Yes, I'm Agent Jesse Meier from the FBI and I would like to ask you some questions, if you don't mind?"

What happened next caught Jesse by surprise. The red-headed man brought his hand from behind him, and Jesse saw the gun that was in his hand and was too slow to react. The man shot Jesse twice in the chest. Agent Jesse was dead before he hit the ground. Anne, hearing the shots, took out her service revolver a moment to slow, as the man shot three shots at her, which missed her twice, but one round hit her in the throat. She grabbed her throat as she shrieked in pain, choking on her own blood, fell to the ground laying on her back with her hand on her neck. She laid there grasping her throat, coughing blood. She opened her eyes as looked up to see the redheaded man with the red beard looking down on her. The man look at her for only a second and took his gun, pointed it at the agent and pulled the trigger.

The man quickly rushed back to the camper. He entered the camper as everyone there was in a panic.

"What the hell happened?" asked Brian.

"Two FBI agents found us. I had to take care of them." Said Shane to Brian as Brian nodded as he understood the situation.

"What do you mean you had to take care of them?" inquired Juan.

Shannon stood there beside Juan, and she knew exactly what her father was saying. She knew he had killed them.

"You know I've had enough of you." said Shane as he lifted his gun and pointed right into Juan's face.

Juan's face changed from a look of disdain to fear. Shannon quickly stepped in front of Juan.

"Get out of my way, woman. I need to take this guy out."

"No, not again. I will not let you kill Juan."

"I said get the hell out of the way, woman."

"You'll have to shoot me first."

Shane lowered his gun in frustration as Brian grabbed his father's arm, and screamed that they had to leave right away, before the cops arrived, and it would pin them in this park. Shane nodded affirmatively as he grabbed a bag out of the back room and told Shannon to come with him right now. She declined to go with her father. He became furious and was ready to cross the room to grab her, but Brian stopped him, saying that Shannon would be safer here that if she was with them. Shane hated the thought, but he knew that his son Brian was right. This wasn't Belfast, they didn't have collaborators to help or shield them. Shannon would be safer here.

The two men left the camper, climbed into their truck, and drove around the crowd of campers and curious onlookers and sped out the park as quickly as they could. They weren't even a block away when they saw a great number of police cars coming towards them as they passed them, heading to the park.

THE CAMPER DOOR SLAMMED as Shane and Brian left. Shannon wrapped her arms around Juan. She had been so petrified that her father was going to kill Juan. They held each other tightly as they heard the truck speed away and the people yelling about the murder of the agents. Juan went to the window, and he saw the crowd gathering. Juan grabbed his computer and quickly placed it in his backpack. He put on his baseball cap, grabbed Shannon's hand, and pulled her to the back of the camper.

"Darling, we have to get out of here as quick as we can, understand?"

"But Juan, the people outside will spot us right away as soon as we go outside."

"We not going out that way."

Shannon had a confused look on her face, not understanding what Juan was talking about. He went to the emergency window that was at the back of the camper and knocked it out. He quickly scurried out, and he then helped Shannon to get out. Juan and Shannon rushed to the damaged area of the fence that surrounded the park. They easily got through the fence as they continued to walk down the road. As they heard police sirens that were sounded louder and louder as they approached the park. A few police cars were coming in the opposite direction from what they were walking, but they continued in the same direction as the cars quickly passed them. The pair didn't stop until they felt they had walked a few miles. They saw some woods ahead and entered it.

AGENT HORTON AND HIS junior agents arrived at the park within an hour. Horton walked to the first body that was covered with a blanket and saw who he knew was agent Anne, even though her face was unrecognizable because of the gunshot wound in her face. He mumbled to himself as Detective Johnson stood quietly behind him. Horton stood up and walked to the second body, uncovering it to look at agent Jesse.

"He never had a chance to take his gun out." Said Johnson.

He looked up at Johnson and asked if they had any idea which way they went?

"No, but I tell you we will know soon. Now that they are out in the open. We'll get these bastards; I promise you that."

Horton stood up. One thing is for sure, he was that he was going to find them and make sure that they would pay for the murder of his agents. Detective Johnson explained that while interrogating some campers, one of them stated he was sure that there were four of them in the camper. He said he was positive there were three men and one red-headed female. We checked the campers and found no one. During the investigation of the camper, one officer noticed they knocked out the emergency window at the back of the camper. After checking the outside of the back of the camper, we found footprints that might be the two that are missing. We also found that in the back of the camper along the back fence there was a break large enough for someone to go through it. Horton nodded and thanked the detective.

Horton turned around and looked at his junior agents. They all looked very confused, like a deer looking into an oncoming headlights. He knew he had to go to them and assure them that this would be avenged. Everyone must work together to accomplish this task. Everyone looked at the other agents as they all agreed. They had to find these guys and stop them for good. He instructed all of them to go back to the station and he joined them as soon as they removed the two bodies. None of them said anything. They just turned around and went to their SUV and left. Horton stood there watching the agents leave as he turned his sight back to the bodies of the dead agents. He felt responsible for the death of these junior agents. The ambulances arrived as they slowly and carefully picked up the agents, placed them in the ambulance, and took them away. Horton stayed a little later as he got all the up to date information of the investigation he could from the team under the direction of Detective Johnson. Johnson was happy to give him information and facts that they had. Horton thanked the detective and left.

SHANE WAS DRIVING NORTH on interstate seventy-five and neither Shane nor Brian said a word.

"Why did you have to shoot the agents?"

"I had no choice but to shoot them. They had found us, and it wouldn't have taken them long to have the area crawling with police."

"Yea, maybe. Said Brian. Now they'll have a score to settle."

"Don't worry. They have to find us first."

Brian nodded. His father was right. But that didn't make Brian feel any more secure about his future. Brian looked at his map and told his father that they were heading toward Sault St-Marie and then Canada. Shane didn't want to go to Canada, so he ask his son what the first main highway west he could take. Brian looked and told his father that the first highway he could see on the map was highway twenty-eight. They could turn there and head west. Brian and his father needed to find a place off the road so they wouldn't be seen and to travel at night until they could find another car. Shane agreed they would find a spot for the night for them to stay and then, hopefully, steal any vehicle that they could find. But first, they needed some supplies. A few miles further, they stopped at a Dollar store and loaded up with some food and munchies. Shane expressed that some beer would be great. Brian was almost sure that they didn't carry any beer.

With supplies loaded up, they continued on a side road until they got to highway twenty-eight and turned left in a westerly direction. They eventually saw a park that was around five miles on highway twenty-eight, so they stopped there until it got dark. They both knew that it was dangerous to drive on the road during daylight. They were sure that there was an all point bulletin out on them and their truck. It wouldn't take long to be spotted. So, they both got out, and sat down at one of the park's picnic table to enjoy some of the food that they got at the Dollar store. As they were enjoying their meal, a very nice black 135 BMW convertible drove into the park. A young man got out of his car, took off his suit jacket and threw it in the back of his car. He bent over, grabbed his bottle of water, and sat down at one of the picnic table with his back to the O'Bradys.

Shane bent over and whispered something into his son's ear. Brian listened attentively as he stared at the young man sitting with his back turned to them. Brian nodded. He understood what his father had told him. Brian stood up and rushed to the young man, screaming.

"Help, help. My father had a heart attack?"

The young man turned around as he saw Brian rushing towards him screaming and pointing back to his father that was slumped over onto the picnic table.

"What happened?"

"I don't know. We were talking, and then he grabbed his chest and collapsed. Please help me."

"Of course, I be glad to help. But I don't know what I can do." They both rushed towards Brian's father.

As they arrived beside the slumped over Shane. He sat up and pointed his gun straight at the young man's chest. The young man stopped immediately and froze in mid-step.

"I appreciate your concern, young man, but I'm doing okay." Before the man said anything, he felt a sharp pain from the back of his head as he collapsed unconscious onto the ground.

"What are we going to do with him?"

"We'll tie and gag him and put him in the woods over there."

"Sounds good. Let's do it."

They quickly tied the man and gagged him.

"Okay, dad. He looks light enough for me to carry him over there."

His father first retrieved the car keys and watched his son pick the man up onto his shoulder. Brought him to the area his father had pointed out and dumped him onto the ground. As Brian was getting rid of the man, Shane was heading to the car, sat in the driver's seat, and waited for Brian to get in, closed the car door and smiled at his father.

"Well, that was nice that God got us a nice car."

They both burst out laughing at the irony of Brian's statement as Shane shifted the car into first gear, second, third and fourth gear in a matter of seconds. They were soon out of sight of the park.

Chapter 18
Canada

Juan and Shannon were still sitting at the restaurant discussing their possible options, on what they should do, and where they would go?

"Maybe we should try to go to Canada."

"I don't think we're in the position to go to Canada. We got Lake Michigan in the way."

"It's only a lake, Juan."

"It is a gigantic lake. It's like a sea."

"Then what are we going to do?"

Juan had a look on his face that, for once in his life, he was uncertain what he was going to do next. He just looked out the window with a large frown covering his face, which slowly changed to a smile. He looked at Shannon, held her hands, and smiled.

"What are you smiling about?"

"Well, my dear, look outside the window and what do you see?"

Shannon glanced out the restaurant window and looked around with a confused look on her face.

"I give up, Juan. What am I supposed to see?

"The bus stop."

"So, what part of the town do you want to go to?"

"That stop is for a Grey Hound bus. They go everywhere in the United States."

"Really, well that changes everything." Said Shannon.

"Wait here." Said Juan.

Shannon watched Juan go to the cashier and speak to the lady. He came back to the table and explained that the bus comes twice a day. Eight in the morning and eight at night. So, there will be one in a few hours. Juan also asked permission for them to stay here until the bus arrives, and she said that it would be okay as long as it didn't get too busy.

As he looked out the window Juan felt that their luck was changing. He just hoped that his luck would continue. He thought if they take the bus to Sault St-Marie they could easily blend into the city. There, he could try to figure out how to cross into Canada and away from the FBI.

A few hours later, when the Greyhound bus finally arrived almost an hour late, Juan and Shannon bought two tickets to Sault St-Marie, found a seat, and sat down near the back of the bus. It only took them a couple of hours to get there. It felt like the bus was stopping at every corner.

"Okay Shannon, wake up. We're here."

Shannon stretched, trying to wake up as she sluggishly got out of her seat and followed Juan out of the bus. The bus station here was bigger than they had thought. As they walked out of the Grey Hound bus terminal, there was a motel across the street from where they were standing. Juan turned and looked at Shannon.

"Well, that is as good a place to stay as any other place. Right?"

"I guess." Said Shannon.

They walked across the street and entered the motel as an elderly gentleman welcomed them to Motel Sault St-Marie. The gentleman asked Juan to sign the register. Juan signed the registry with Mr. and Mrs. Juan Rodriques. The man read the register and then welcomed us as Mr. and Mrs. Rodrigues. Shannon looked at me but thankfully decided not to say anything until we entered the room. The room was fairly small, with one double bed. Shannon looked at Juan as he looked back with a huge smile of excitement surging through his body.

"Really, Juan? Just because we're going to die in a hail of bullets at any moment doesn't mean..."

"Doesn't a dying man deserve a last request before the sentence is served?"

Shannon gave a stare that might have caused frostbite throughout his body.

"Okay, okay, and I'll sleep on that chair."

Shannon smiled at Juan and went across the room to give him a nice, passionate kiss. Juan suggested they go out for supper before they turned in. Shannon agreed.

IT WAS GETTING LATE when Shane saw a gas station ahead, so he stopped. The car definitely needed some gas. Brian told his father since they were here, they might as well get something to eat at the adjoining restaurant called C&G's Family Restaurant. Shane agreed and told him he would meet him in the restaurant as soon as he finished. They showed Brian to a booth near the back of the restaurant. Finally, Shane came in and sat across from Brian.

"What took you so long?"

"I had to do something first."

"Yes what?"

"I switched the plates on the BMW with a Volkswagen bus."

"Great thinking, dad."

They sat there finishing their beers as the server, Giselle asked them if they would be interested in a dessert. They answered they were having their dessert now, and they were ready for a refill. The server came back with two more coronas with a slice of lime.

"Here's to you dad, may we live long enough to get back to Ireland?"

"Yes son, to Ireland."

Before they left, they finished a few more beers. They weren't feeling any pain. Brian suggested they get a room at the motel down the street. His father agreed he was in no condition to do any driving.

JUAN TOSSED AND TURNED in the most uncomfortable chair in the whole dam world as far as he was concerned. He tried to sit up as a sharp pain went across his lower back.

"Ouch, my dam back."

"Juan, why don't you come lie beside me?"

Juan nodded okay as he got up from the terrible chair and lay down beside Shannon. Shannon gave him a look and told him to behave, or he would be back in his chair. Juan was okay with her condition. His back couldn't handle another minute in that chair. It didn't take Juan much time to fall asleep. He was snoring and kept Shannon awake most of the night, regretting her decision to let Juan get in the bed beside her.

Juan woke up as he rubbed his back. That was still hurting. He stared at Shannon that had finally fallen asleep, even with his snoring. Juan just laid there as he continued to look at her beautiful face. She slowly woke up and stretched again to wake up her exhausted body.

"Good morning, darling."

"Ah, I feel like I could sleep for a week."

"You hungry?"

"Yes, I am. Breakfast would be great."

"Well, let's get some. There has to be a restaurant near here."

As they exited the motel, Juan saw a Waffle house down the street, so they headed in that direction. As they approached the restaurant, they noticed three police cars in the parking lot, so they did an about face and tried to find another restaurant. They couldn't find one, so they went to the gas station that had everything from personal pizza, subs, and sandwiches. So, they both got a six-inch sub, chips and soft drinks and headed back to their room. The room had a small desk that they used as a table. Juan brought around the chair for Shannon as he sat down on the bed. Before he sat down, Juan opened the television and found a news channel. They listened to the news broadcaster for a few minutes while they ate. Then they stopped when they heard the broadcaster say,

"News about the assassin of the two FBI that were assassinated at the state park is still unknown. The perpetrators could escape. There is presently an APB on the two men suspected in the assassination of the FBI agents. Reports on the two men is one man is a large approximately two hundred and fifty pounds, six feet, and six inches tall with red hair to his shoulders, and a long fiery red beard. The second man is also red headed but with short hair and I believe him to be around six feet tall and around one hundred and eighty pounds. If you see anyone that is similar, please notify this hot-line 1 999-200-2000. The FBI insists we stress the importance of caution. They are very dangerous.

Now for the weather report, there is a large pressure area ..."

Juan had turned off the television and saw that Shannon was very upset on what she heard on the television about her father and brother.

"It will be okay. Your father and brother have gone through this before. They know how to get around this mess."

"I know that they have been in this type of scenario before. But now they are involved with the FBI. Those guys don't fool around and now that they've killed two of them, they will want revenge for their fallen comrades."

He nodded. He understood and agreed with what Shannon was saying. The FBI now would be after them, and they would not be interested in talking, but a thirst for blood. Shannon walked towards Juan as he wrapped his arms around her to console her. They realized that the FBI's thirst for blood meant it was probably only a matter of time before they killed them. Juan stood there, holding Shannon tightly as she looked at him.

"I love you Shannon. I promise you we will get out of this mess. "

Shannon kissed Juan and told him she loved him as well. But she wasn't convinced of how they could get out of the United States. Juan just smiled at her, and he said that he was working on an idea that he plans to put in effect this evening. They have to be ready to move at their first opportunity.

"Okay, Juan, I'll be ready when you want me to be."

Juan smiled and got their stuff ready to leave.

"There is a truck stop near here maybe with a little bit of luck we'll be able to get a ride?"

THE YOUNG MAN AT THE reception desk was just starting his night shift when the O'Bradys walked in and were getting their room from Mr. Stamos, the daytime receptionist.

"Well, Mr. Stamos, it looks like they've been partying."

"Yes, it sure does, John. I hope they don't cause you any problems. That big guy with a red beard is huge."

"You're right. That guy's muscles have muscles."

Both of them chuckled, as the young man said goodnight to Mr. Stamos as he left.

Both Shane and Brian collapsed on their bed as the room spun around.

"Brian, we got to get out of here in the morning."

"Okay."

They were both asleep in minutes. Their snoring could be heard throughout the motel.

The young man at the reception desk was just starting his night shift when the O'Brady walked in and were getting their room from Mr. Stamos, the daytime receptionist. He hoped that Mr. Stamos was correct and that they wouldn't cause any problems during his night shift. He was hoping to catch up with his statistics homework. He hated statistics; it was very hard for him to understand. Most of this stuff was way above his abilities, but he had to understand it. He needed it to get his degree. He grabbed his chair and laid his statistic book on the counter as he picked up the TV remote and turned on the television. He opened his book to chapter 13, which he felt was a bad omen.

He read the first problem and became overwhelmed before he started. Frustrated, he sat back in his chair and grabbed his soda and took a drink. He looked up at the television that was mounted on the wall as the newscaster came on. The Newscaster was talking about the lack of any updates on the two fugitives that the FBI was searching for. He then proceeded again to describe the two men that were named Shane and Brian O'Donovan. He also stressed that they considered both these men extremely dangerous. That there was now a one hundred thousand dollar reward for their capture. He then said that if you have any information about these fugitive, call the FBI hotline 1-999-200-2000.

John stood up and turned the registration book around and looked at the signature of the two guys that had just registered. He couldn't believe it. The men must have not realized under their intoxication that they printed their actual name, Shane, and Brian O'Donovan. That was the name that the news broadcaster said and these guys sure fitted the description. John sat back in his chair thinking of the reward. It would pay for his schooling. John picked up his phone and entered the number.

An FBI agent answered the call immediately.

"FBI hotline. Who am I speaking to?"

"My name is John Booth."

"What is your phone number in case we get disconnected?"

"It's area code 231-528-1976"

"Thank you. Do you have any information on the two fugitive?"

"Yes, I work at Trail motel on State Highway M28. I have two clients that fit the description of the two men that I heard on the news."

The FBI agents gave a detailed description of the two fugitive in question. The young motel receptionist answered yes to every descriptive question. John hung up with the FBI. He then patiently waited for the FBI to show up as the agent had stated.

Around two AM, a large unit of the FBI team showed up. They armed themselves with high-powered weapons, body armor, and night vision glasses. The first agent quietly walked into the motel entrance as he motioned to the clerk to keep quiet. He waved the fellow agents ahead down the hallway and with weapons drawn and pointing toward the door. They waited for instructions to enter the room and engage the perpetrators. John covered his ears as overpowering sounds of gunfire pierced his ears. John was about to find out that Shane and Brian O'Donovan were both dead. The FBI team had successfully taken down the two perpetrators. John was relieved but still shaken by the events that had just transpired. The FBI agents were kind and understanding, allowing him to process the situation. They asked him a few questions and offered support. After a few hours, with the bodies of Shane and Brian O'Donovan removed, the FBI agents left. They left John alone with his thoughts. He was relieved but saddened by the events that had taken place. He had no clue what would happen next, but he knew he had to stay strong and continue to move forward in life. He had to remember that this was not his fault; it was the fault of the two perpetrators and the life they led.

Chapter 19
Sault Ste-Marie

THE PAST EVENTS SPED through Juan's mind as he remembered that he and Shannon sprinted through the dense forest, their hearts were pounding with fear and adrenaline. They had to keep moving if they wanted to escape the FBI agents they knew would be hot on their heels.

Only a few hours earlier, they had been holed up at the Ignace State Park with Shannon's father and brother, Shane, and Brian. But everything changed when Shane and Brian carried out a daring assassination of two FBI agents who had been closing in on them.

Juan had been the only one to witness the gruesome act and had quickly alerted Shannon, urging her to run with him before they too were caught in the crossfire. And now, with the sound of helicopters overhead and dogs barking in the distance, their only hope was to disappear. They tried to go through this area of woods, but the terrain was rough and unforgiving, and they stumbled more than once, almost giving themselves away to possible authorities that might be on their trail. Juan's heart was pounding with every step, his mind racing with the possibilities of what could happen if they were caught.

They finally came to a clearing, and Shannon's eyes widened as she spotted a small cabin nestled among the trees. "Over there!" she shouted to Juan, and they made a mad dash for the cabin's door. No one was home and the door wasn't lock that surprised Juan.

Once inside, they quickly barricaded themselves inside, hoping that the agents wouldn't find them. But they knew that it was only a matter of time before the FBI closed in on them.

As they waited in the dimly lit cabin, their nerves frayed with fear and uncertainty, Juan and Shannon knew that they had to come up with a plan to escape. The odds were stacked against them, but they refused to give up without a fight.

And so, they hatched a plan to sneak out of the cabin under the cover of darkness and make their way to the nearby town, where they hoped to find help and refuge.

But as they crept through the woods, Juan and Shannon knew that the FBI could watch their every move. Juan was sure that they were closing in on them with every passing moment. Their fate was uncertain, but they refused to give up hope.

Juan and Shannon navigate the treacherous terrain to evade any FBI agents or police. None were coming.

THEY FINALLY REACHED a truck stop

Shannon spoke to Juan "are you okay?"

"Yes why do you ask?"

"I don't know what happened to you."

"What do you mean?"

"It looked like you were in a daze. I spoke to you, and you didn't answer me."

"Sorry. I was thinking of our past events."

"Stay here I'll be right back."

For the first time in a long while, they felt a glimmer of hope.

"What are we going to do now Juan?"

"We are going to sneak into Canada."

"But I don't have a passport. Mine is still in the camper at St Ignace state Park."

"So, is mine."

"We have to be careful," Juan whispered to Shannon. "We don't know if the FBI has alerted Canadian authorities yet."

Shannon nodded, her eyes scanning the area for any signs of trouble. As they waited in line with the other vehicles, they noticed an open-ended semi-truck parked a few feet away. It seemed to be unattended, and they both saw an opportunity.

"Let's try to hide in there," Shannon said, nodding towards the truck.

Juan hesitated for a moment, not sure if it was a good idea. But he knew that they couldn't afford to take any chances. "Okay," he said finally, "Let's do it."

They quickly made their way towards the semi-truck, praying that it was empty. As they got closer, they could see that it was piled high with boxes and crates, creating a labyrinth of hiding places.

Without hesitation, they climbed up into the back of the truck, quickly finding a hiding spot behind a stack of crates. As they crouched down, they could hear the sounds of vehicles passing through the customs checkpoint, the voices of customs officials echoing through the air.

Their hearts were pounding with fear as they waited, not knowing if they would be discovered. But after what felt like an eternity, the sound of the customs officials faded away, and the truck began to move.

Juan and Shannon exchanged a look of relief, knowing that they had made it through undetected. As the truck rumbled through the streets of Sault Ste. Marie, they knew that they still had a long road ahead of them. But for the first time in a long while, they felt a glimmer of hope that they might make it to safety after all.

Juan and Shannon finally had the chance to get out of the truck when it finally reached Toronto. They quickly scurried out of their hiding place in the semi-truck and were out of site of the truck depot within minutes. It was getting late, and they knew they had to get some food and lodging. They stopped at a LaFleur hot dog stand and had a few steamy hot dogs with mustard, onions, and coleslaw, greasy fries, and a Pepsi. They gobbled down the food like there was no tomorrow.

After devouring their meal at the LaFleur hot dog stand, Juan and Shannon felt their energy levels finally start to rise. They knew they still had a long way to go, but at least they wouldn't be traveling on empty stomachs.

As they walked through the streets of Toronto, they scanned the area for any signs of danger. They knew that they were still being hunted by the FBI, and that they couldn't afford to let their guard down.

Eventually, they came across a small motel on the outskirts of the city. It wasn't much, but it would have to do. They paid for a room in cash, not wanting to leave any digital trail behind.

As they settled into the room, exhaustion washed over them. They had been on the run for days, and they were both starting to feel the strain.

"Juan," Shannon said, breaking the silence, "What are we going to do now?"

Juan sighed, his mind racing with possibilities. He knew that they couldn't stay in Toronto for long. They would need to keep moving, stay one step ahead of the FBI.

"I don't know," he said finally. "But we'll figure something out. We have to."

Shannon nodded, looking up at him with a fierce determination in her eyes. "We'll make it through this," she said, "Together."

And with those words, they both knew that they had a fighting chance. They didn't know what the future held, but they knew that they would face it together, no matter what.

They laid in bed in each other's arms in embrace of passion. As their lust for each other was overwhelming and beyond eithers control they both reached a level of climax that neither had ever reached. Juan slid off Shannon sweaty body as he held here closely ever so closely as they embraced, and Shannon laid her lips on Juan and said.

"I love you Juan."

"I know Shannon," As Juan smiled.

Shannon giggled as she laid her face on Juan's still wet chest.

They both fell asleep in each other's arms.

The next morning Juan and Shannon got up and left the motel after they asked the attendant where the best place was, for a cheap breakfast. He suggested that they go to Christos Café about a quarter of a mile north of there. Juan thanked the man as Shannon smiled at him as they left the motel.

They entered the restaurant and were brought to their table as Juan grabbed himself a copy of the Toronto Star. The server was there immediately, as she asked if they were ready to give their choice from the breakfast menu while she poured them both a cup of coffee.

Juan asked the server what she would suggest, and she immediately came out with the Christo's Greek dish.

"Sounds good. What is it?" asked Juan.

The server explained in detail a large omelet with onions, green peppers, and Feta cheese and two large pancakes with Quebec Maple Syrup if they would like.

Both said yes. That sounded great!

Juan grabbed the newspaper he had taken and opened it to the front page. His eyes widened as the smile left his face.

On the front page was the photos of Shane and Brian O'Brady that was now named O'Donovan.

Two Propagators Who Were Responsible for The Assassination of Two FBI Agents shot Dead!

Cited

Https://www.makeuseof.com/tag/most-famous-computer-viruses/[1]

---

1. https://www.makeuseof.com/tag/most-famous-computer-viruses/

Don't miss out!

Visit the website below and you can sign up to receive emails whenever Panayotis publishes a new book. There's no charge and no obligation.

https://books2read.com/r/B-A-SIDW-SAMIC

BOOKS 2 READ

Connecting independent readers to independent writers.

Did you love *White-Noise Conspiracy*? Then you should read *Michael*[2] by Panayotis!

The nightmare sucks you down. Down to a place never before seen by man. You go deeper and deeper into the underworld ...

---

2. https://books2read.com/u/bONeoA

3. https://books2read.com/u/bONeoA

Also by Panayotis

Junior and Dumb Old Bo
Junior and Dumb Old Bo
Junior and Dumb Old Bo's Trip To The Olympics

Standalone
Michael
White-Noise Conspiracy

About the Author

<u>The Author</u>

Panayotis, presently living in Lakewood Ranch, Florida. He is married to the love of his life Susan and has three sons. Jesse, Andrew, and Junior. He retired as a Registered Respiratory Therapist in 2014. This is Panayoti's second book in the *Junior and Dumb Old Bo* series. Panayotis is working on his third book, "Michael" which he hopes to finish soon.